WITH *her*

ENTWINED IN YOU BOOK FIVE
ASHLEE ROSE

Cover by Irish Ink
Formatting by Irish Ink

Editing by Karen Sanders Editing

I hope my book helps you to escape reality for a while

- Stay safe, lots of love xo.

OTHER BOOKS BY ASHLEE ROSE

ENTWINED IN YOU SERIES

Something New

Something To Lose

Something Everlasting

Before Her

All available on Amazon Kindle Unlimited

Only suitable for 18+ due to nature of the books.

CHAPTER ONE

I drove away, keeping my eyes on her in my rear-view mirror as I did. As soon as she was out of sight, I pulled my eyes back to the road, not looking back. My heart slowly broke piece by piece as I left her in Jake's. This is what I wanted. I wanted to break her heart and completely ruin her, but I should have stopped when I fell for her, yet I just couldn't stay away. I wanted to turn around, beg for her to forgive me, but I was too proud to do that. I felt like hell; I didn't even know how she felt. She would never forgive me, and I didn't blame her. I was angry. So angry with myself and what I had planned.

Of course it was going to come out. Of course I was going to hurt her. I should have been a man and told her, told her my intentions, but I was too much of a pussy to be straight up and honest. Now I had to deal with the consequences. I needed to try and get her back, but I was too ashamed to do that now. I needed to go to New York, get back into my business mind then try to work my way back to her. It wasn't going to be easy, but I knew she was my soulmate and we were destined to be together. I just wished I could turn back time and stop this from happening. All this overthinking wouldn't change anything. I just needed to give her time. Give myself time to work out exactly what I was going to do. I was pulled from my thoughts when I heard a car horn. My car was veering onto the other side of the road towards oncoming traffic. I swerved and tried to calm my breathing. *Concentrate, Carter*! I took a few deep breaths before turning Linkin Park's *Numb* up so loud I could feel the drums beating through me. It felt amazing to let the music drown out my thoughts. I needed to get home and to New York.

I would get her back if it was the last thing I did. I wouldn't give up. Even if it took me years, she would be mine, and once I had her, I'd never let her go again.

.

CHAPTER TWO

I let out a relieved sigh as I stepped off my private jet. New York was non-stop from the moment I landed. But it was good for my mind. I was out there for four weeks in total. Not as long as I first anticipated, but it still felt like a lifetime that I was away from Freya. I had tried calling her a few times while I was out there and sent numerous messages, only for her to ignore me. I promised myself I would try a couple more times, and if I got nothing, I would leave her be. As they say, '*if you love something, let it go. If it comes back, then that's how you know*'. I just needed to trust that fate had this all mapped out for me. I would get her back, it was just going to take time. I nodded at James as I slid into the car.

"James." I smiled at him. I had missed him and Julia.

"Carter, how was your trip?" he asked me as he sat in the front and started to drive.

"Exhausting, to be honest, mate," I said quietly. "But I am glad to be home." I scrolled through the hundreds of unread emails I didn't need. I'm sure people just liked copying me in for fun. I rolled my eyes before putting my phone inside my suit pocket.

"No news on Freya?" he asked, his eyes boring into mine in the rear-view mirror.

"Nope. Nothing. I'm not giving up though. There will come a time when I run into her and try to get her back." I nodded confidently.

"You will get your chance." He smiled at me. "I have a good feeling about this." He nodded at his own comment.

I wished I could see into the future and see if he was right. As much as I didn't want to give up, there might come a time when I may have to. I thought about moving to Elsworth and just waiting until I bumped into her, but then I would seem like an obsessed stalker. There had been so many ideas running through my head, but I wanted to give her space. I wanted her to know I was never going to push her into something she didn't want. If she didn't want me, as much as it would completely crush me, I would never chase her. But I wasn't ready to give up yet.

With that, I pulled my phone out, clicking my recent phone numbers. There hers was, my beautiful Freya. I clicked her number, smiling weakly at the photo of us on her contact image. It was a photo from Laura and Tyler's wedding. She always looked beautiful, but she was glowing. I liked to think I made her feel that way, that I gave her that glow, because she gave me a glow like no one else ever had.

I felt my throat tighten as the burn crawled up, causing a lump to form. I rubbed my eyes then coughed, clearing my throat. I didn't want to attract James' attention. I clicked her number. I'm sure my heart stopped beating as the phone rang. And like every other time I called her, it went to her voicemail;

'Hi, this is Freya. I'm sorry I can't come to the phone at the moment. Please leave a message after the beep and I'll call you back.'

I smiled at her voice. God, I missed her voice. I missed everything about her. The beep echoed through my ears when I realized I had let it go further than I ever had before.

"Er, erm, hi, Freya. It's me. Carter." I coughed. "Please call me back. I have tried to give you time. I tried my best not to contact you while I was away in New York, but you haven't left my mind since I left you in Elsworth. I should have never driven away and I regret that moment every second of every day. You were everything to me, and I know I fucked it up and I can never say sorry enough, but I truly am. I truly am sorry. This will be the last time I will call. I will give you your space. We will find each other. It may be next week, it may be in ten years, but I know we will find each other again and be together forever. I really am sorry. I love you forever and always."

11

I had to stop, my eyes brimming with tears, my voice betraying me and showing her exactly how vulnerable I felt.

"*Always mine. Always my Freya,*" I whispered before cutting the phone off.

I put my hand up to my face, running my thumb and finger across my brows, shielding my eyes from James as a single tear fell from my empty sage eyes. I was broken. I couldn't lie to myself anymore. I thought I was feeling a little bit more human after New York, but the truth was, I was just pushing my feelings down as far as they would go.

I turned my phone off for the rest of the journey. We only had a short way left, but I didn't want to be tempted to text or call her again. I wanted to take my suit off and let the hot water of the shower run over my body.

A sigh of relief left my lungs when we pulled into the penthouse car park. I hadn't been back to the townhouse since Freya. I couldn't face it without her. If we did get back together, we would start afresh. I wouldn't live in the penthouse with her. I don't want her to be reminded of my previous life—our previous life—and all the mistakes I made to get us to where we were today.

I thanked James as I walked towards the lift of the penthouse, dragging my suitcase behind me. I relieved James of his duties for the afternoon, and once I'd had dinner, I'd relieve Julia. I dropped my suitcase to the floor. I would normally unpack, but I felt physically and mentally exhausted. I wasn't sure if it was the jetlag kicking in, or just being back there, but I felt like a tremendous weight had just crashed down on me. My heart was shattered. I felt completely broken. I walked up to my room and straight into my en-suite. I peeled my suit off and discarded it to the floor. I didn't have the energy to even throw it in the wash basket. Julia would understand. I was never like this, but I just needed to shower, eat, and sleep.

I stood under the scalding hot water, feeling the tension slowly leave my body as the water turned my tanned skin slightly red. I felt like it was washing all the bad out of my body. I wished it was, but I could never rid the bad that lay in me. It's who I am. It's part of my make-up, my DNA. I didn't deserve to be happy. I didn't deserve her.

After spending far too long under the shower, I dragged my sorry arse out and towelled myself down. I stared at myself in the mirror; I looked like a broken man. My stubble was coming through, and my eyes were dull and lifeless. I felt like letting myself go. I was in a mood and I needed to shake it. Normally, I would call one of my girls, but I couldn't. I couldn't be with another woman until I knew that I'd tried everything to get Freya back. If, and it was a big if, she didn't come back to me then I would need to let her go. But it hadn't come to that yet.

I felt so frustrated with pent up emotion. I needed a drink, but first I wanted to lie down, try and calm my thoughts. All I could think of was her. She was imprinted on my brain. She may as well have been tattooed on my eyelids as every time I closed my goddamn eyes, she was there. My heart was breaking a little more each day knowing I'd hurt her, that I broke her completely. She trusted me. She may have even started to love me after what Jake did to her. Then I came along, gave her new hope that I was going to make her happy, and God did I enjoy making her happy, but then I fucked it up. Because of some spoilt brat who wanted more with me. Wanted the lifestyle more like. If she truly wanted me, she would have worked a little harder when I put my barriers up that morning in the kitchen when I pushed her away. But fuck, I am so glad I pushed her away because in doing so, I met the love of my life. I fell hard and fast for her. I was a sucker when it came to her. I thought I fell hard with Rylie. Shit, I wish. Rylie was nothing compared to Freya. Freya was a queen; Rylie was merely a peasant who played me like a puppet.

I pushed my hand through my hair as I felt the anger start to rise from the pit of my stomach. I needed to lash out, but I had no one to lash out on. I stood from the bed, the towel dropping to my feet before I paced up and down my room like a mad man. I didn't know what I was doing, but I needed to shake my anger. I needed to calm the fuck down, but I felt like I had gone past the point of calm. I had seen red. The sad thing is, I was only angry at myself. For letting this go on for as long as it did.

I stopped dead and stared at the floor length mirror in my walk-in wardrobe, ashamed of myself and my behaviour. I strolled towards it, lifting my hand up behind my shoulder and balling my fist, ready to obliterate the mirror like I obliterated Freya's heart, but I couldn't. It was as if she was in my head, telling me to walk away. I was good at that, walking away. I dropped my arm in defeat, turning on my heel and walking back towards my bedroom before falling into my bed. I was mentally exhausted. Heartbroken and empty. My soul felt like it had left my body and was roaming around, waiting for its destined soulmate. I was a lost soul, waiting for her to come and find me again. Waiting for her to accept me back into her heart so our souls could entwine once more, and this time, not break.

How the fuck could I have been so stupid to blow this? I had no right to love her. Had no right to want her to forgive me. I ruined it. I ruined her. I ruined us.

My last chance of my happily ever after. My head was telling me it was over, my heart begging me not to give in and to keep fighting for her. There was no going back. I felt like we were destined to fail. Yet, I still didn't want to give up. And I wouldn't, until she told me face to face she didn't want me anymore.

CHAPTER THREE

All the days of the past month had rolled into one. I still had no word from Freya. My heart was completely shattered. I couldn't function. I had one last attempt to get her to listen. If she still didn't respond then I would leave her be. I couldn't put myself through the torture anymore. It wasn't like I'd been happy and I was now going to be miserable. I had been miserable since the nineteenth of August.

Winter was threatening to start, another season gone with no word from her at all. She was like a ghost. She was nowhere to be seen on social media. I tried reaching out to Laura, but she ghosted me, understandably. I didn't have to courage to contact Rose or Harry. He would have my balls if I contacted him. I sighed as I looked at the time on my Rolex. I had an hour before I was meeting him. Ethan. Even the thought of his name left a sour taste on my tongue. I knew she would listen to him. There was something between them I could never understand. But I needed to trust him. I needed to know he wouldn't fuck this up for me. Plus, he was loved up with some waitress, so I had no worries about him going after Freya... I hoped.

I styled my hair then rubbed my hand against my long stubble. I debated shaving, but to be honest, I quite liked the rugged look. My appearance had been the last thing on my mind. I didn't have to see anyone; I'd only been into the office a handful of times. I couldn't face the dipshits I worked with. I hadn't got the patience. I grabbed my Harrington jacket before making my way downstairs. I didn't even look at Julia. I didn't want to make small talk. Before disappearing, I stopped at my office and re-read the letter I had written for Freya; the letter that would be going to Ethan.

Freya,

I am sorry for this letter, but this is the only way I knew you would listen, especially when Ethan gave it to you.

I know I have said this over and over again in the text messages and voicemail, but I really am sorry. Yes, my intention was to get revenge, but as soon as I saw your beautiful face, that revenge left. I fell in love with you. I have never felt this way about anyone.

Let me fill you in on what happened that has led us to this:

Aimee was, in fact, one of my girls. There was

something about her that made me think I wanted more. She was unlike the other girls. I started to develop feelings for her, but she was never interested in me like that. It was all about the money with her. I am laughing to myself as I'm writing this as I was stupid enough to not realize her ways at the time. She started acting weird, missing her shifts. I started to get suspicious, so I had someone follow her, which led me to Jake. It seemed that Aimee and Jake had been having an affair for a while, which you knew. (I am not a stalker, I promise, I just have contacts, you know... if ever needed) I was so angry with everything that I started looking into Jake's life. That's when I came across you. Beautiful you. I thought if I started something with you, Jake would feel how I felt when I found out about him and Aimee. But he didn't. I felt the hurt, the heartbreak, the loss. I should have told you about this on our first date, but then again, at the time I didn't see myself falling for you as hard as I did.

I know me explaining it probably doesn't make it any better, but I just wanted you to know my reasons.

I love you, Freya. With all my heart. Even though I feel like I have no right to love you, because it was me who chose to walk away from you when I could have stayed there and tried to make this right.

I feel like I have no right to miss you, even though I do. My heart feels like it's been shattered into a thousand pieces. I feel empty without you.

Freya, I still love you, more than you will ever know.

I wish I could see you, smell you, hear your voice, and kiss you one more time, because I would make sure I remembered every single detail.

I hope you get to read this. I haven't stopped thinking about you. Take all the time you need with work. If you want to leave, I will understand. You honestly were my everything, Freya. I was stupid to throw it away over something that I realize meant nothing to me.

No one will ever take your place. I promise.

Love you always, Carter X

I let out the breath I had been holding in. This was it. My last attempt to get through to her. I placed the letter back in its envelope, tucking the flap inside it before staring at the front, her name simply written: '*Freya*'.

I grabbed my phone off charge before walking to the elevator and going down to the basement to get in my car. I put my foot down hard on the accelerator, making my wheels spin on the tarmac and making them screech, echoing through the car park. I lost myself to my music as I made my way to the coffee shop near Freya's flat. I knew she wasn't there. She was at her mum and dad's; Ethan told me. I would have done anything to run up to her door and bang on it until she had to answer. I sighed as I pulled into a space outside the coffee shop. I turned the engine off and just sat quietly for a moment, calming my breathing. My heart was thumping against my ribcage. I felt like it was trying to leap from my chest. I took one last deep breath before leaving my safe place. I felt exposed. I readjusted my belt on my jeans and made sure my polo shirt was untucked. Not sure why I was making sure I looked half decent, it was only Ethan. But I had to be prepared for the what if. What if she was sitting next to him? What if he didn't tell her he was meeting me but just invited her down for coffee and a catch up? The thoughts plagued my mind, which then caused my heart to start racing. I didn't know what I would do if I saw her. What would I say?

Calm down, big guy. It's just Ethan. The curly-haired fuck you disliked only a few months ago.

I smiled as the thoughts of Ethan came flooding through. God, he wanted her so bad, but she wanted me. To be honest, maybe she would have been better with him. He wouldn't have done this to her. He wouldn't have broken her like I did in the small amount of time I knew her. I was selfish and greedy, stealing her from a happy relationship for my own gains. I actually disgusted myself. I patted my jacket, making sure the letter was still in there, and thank God, it was. I silenced my phone and slid it into my Levi's back pocket. I locked my Maserati and walked into the coffee shop, searching for Ethan. It didn't take long to seek out his hazel eyes and curly mop of hair. He smiled weakly at me. As I approached him, he leant across and patted me on the back. "Carter," he said in a hushed voice.

"Ethan," I replied with a clipped tone. "Do you want another coffee?"

"Yeah, mate. Black Americano, please," he said as he took his seat again.

"No problem," I said before walking up to the counter. I stood quietly, waiting for the barista to call me forward. It felt like I was waiting ages. I just wanted to get this sorted and done. I didn't want to be sitting there for hours, pouring my heart out to Ethan over my failed relationship with someone he wanted as much as I did.

I smiled weakly as the barista called me forward, handing my cash over as I ordered our two Americanos. I waited a couple of minutes then was handed the steaming hot black coffee. The strong scent filling my nose was good. I didn't realise how much I needed this. My sleep had been awful ever since I left Freya.

I walked over to the table with our cups, placing them both on the table.

"Here you go," I said, passing him his cup before sitting down opposite him. I adjusted uncomfortably in my seat as I waited for him to start a conversation, but he just stared me down, obviously waiting for me to say something.

I rolled my eyes, letting out a pissed off sigh. "So, have you spoken to her?" I said bluntly as I lifted the hot coffee to my lips and letting the smooth brown liquid slide down my throat. It was good.

"Yeah, I have." He nodded before taking a sip of his own

coffee.

"I know it's a stupid question, but how is she?" I winced as I asked him.

"How do you think she is?" he snapped, obviously a rhetorical question. "She is completely broken, Carter. How could you do that to her? I thought you were a good guy." He sighed, shaking his head.

If I didn't need his help so much, I would have punched him straight in his smug little face.

"I did say it was a stupid question," I replied with a snarky tone, biting the inside of my mouth to stop myself from flipping. "I didn't mean to hurt her, you know that, yeah?"

"Well, when I first met you, I would've said you were talking shit, but I saw you two together. I knew you had something. I just don't understand how this happened." His eyes narrowed as he focused on me.

"I was a pussy who couldn't tell her the fucking truth. Look where it's got me. Heartbroken and a mess. I couldn't give two fucks if I don't wake up in the morning. She is the reason I exist. I was put on this Earth for her and no one else," I said, flitting my eyes down to my coffee. "I don't deserve her." The words left my lips in a whisper.

"You're right, you don't," Ethan snapped. I flicked my eyes up to him. They were now full of anger as I focused on his punchable face. "But," he said calmly, holding his hand up, "I will do everything I can to help you. Because she is miserable without you. She has lost weight, and her glow has gone. She gets up, cries, eats, cries, and sleeps. I honestly don't know what to do. Her mum is at a loose end, Harry is furious, and Laura just wants to be there for her but she hasn't been well so Freya has been dealing with this on her own." He swallowed. "I can't even get through to her, to be honest. I don't know if she will listen to me when I see her tomorrow. I just hope for your sake your letter is good." He smirked at me.

"I don't even know if it's good. You're welcome to read it. I basically explained why I did what I did. Not that it makes it any better, but I hope it helps her understand," I said as I reached into my pocket and held it out in front of me. I was so reluctant to hand it over to him, but I knew I had to. If I had any chance of her listening to me, this was it. This was that moment. I passed it over to him and let go as he took it from me and placed it in his coat pocket.

"I'm rooting for you, Carter, I really am. I'll text you when I get there. I'll delete our messages 'cos I know her. She will no doubt go through my phone and try and have a snoop." He laughed slightly.

"Thanks, Ethan. I really do appreciate it. When you cuddle her, cuddle her from me, please," I said quietly.

"No problem. I'll be in touch," he said as he finished his coffee and stood up. "Take care, Carter." He placed his hand on my shoulder and squeezed it slightly as he walked past me.

I didn't know if I was doing the right thing or not, but it was done. This was the moment of truth.

***

Saturday evening soon came around. I sat looking at my phone all day, staring at Freya's name, praying she text or called me. Just as I was about to give up and accept defeat, my phone lit up, and Ethan's name flashed across it. My heart was thumping so fucking hard it felt like it was skipping beats. My throat felt tight. I stared at my screen, not doing anything for the moment. I was mentally preparing myself for what he might have to say. After a few moments, I unlocked my phone, sliding my thumb across the message notification;

It's Freya. I got your letter from Ethan. Thanks for clearing that up.

That was it. That was all she could give me after I explained everything. I was broken, and this was the final nail in the coffin. She had destroyed all hope in that one text message. I was done. I locked my phone screen and threw it at the wall, my anger taking over before I realized what I had done. I jumped down from the bar stool, picking it up and looking at the damage I had caused. I had completely shattered it. The screen flickered. It was like a broken jigsaw puzzle. Bits of the display were jumbled, and I couldn't make sense of any of it. In that moment, I dropped my phone to the floor. I felt deflated as I slid down the kitchen units. I had come undone by her message. It couldn't be over. I couldn't lose her. But it was too late. I had lost her, and she didn't want me back. I didn't have the energy to try anymore.

I closed my eyes, and like always, her beautiful face graced my thoughts. Her long, auburn hair that made her grey eyes pop. Her tanned skin that always glowed when she was with me. Her plump lips she used to sink her perfectly white teeth into, used to kiss me with. I missed the sound of my name rolling off her tongue, her moans as I made her feel so overwhelmed with pleasure and love. The flashbacks were pure ecstasy, and like the addict she had made me, she was all I craved. I hadn't noticed the tears were pooling. My eyes stung as the tears threatened to come, even though I tried everything to stop them. The lump in my throat was burning where I needed to just let go. I needed to let myself crumble and give in to the tears. All it took was one blink, one blink giving my body the go ahead to release the tears I had been hiding for so long. The tears that had been wanting to leave since my heart was broken into a million pieces, and it was all because of my selfish ways. My chest hurt, and my ribs felt like they were crushing around my heart. I was scared I wouldn't wake in the morning. I was scared I was going to die from a broken heart. You hear that, don't you? People dying of broken hearts. I always thought it was a load of bollocks, but now I was going through it. I could see it was true, because my heart was broken, and I honestly didn't think I could go on. I laid myself down on my cold, tiled kitchen floor, staring at my phone. My eyes were dry. I had no more tears to cry, but the pain in my hollow chest was unbearable. I fisted my polo shirt as I clung to it, trying to ease the pain when my eyes started closing. I couldn't do anything to stop the heaviness; this was it. I was succumbing to my heartbreak. I saw my phone flicker with life. I slid my hand out and pulled it towards me before my eyes closed completely. I saw her name. I'm sure it was her name, or was it just my mind playing tricks on me?

Before I could try and look again, I gave into the darkness.

Broken. Exhausted. Ruined.

CHAPTER FOUR

I couldn't open my eyes, as much as I tried with all my might. I knew I was exhausted, but I was scared too. Scared of so many things, like a terrified boy trapped in a never-ending nightmare. All of a sudden, Freya walked towards me looking like the perfect angel she was. Her long auburn hair was curled to perfection; it fell down her back and sat just under her rounded breast. She wore a long, white maxi dress. She reminded me of a Greek goddess. Her skin was aglow, as if her aura was penetrating throughout her soul. Her aura lit up, seeking me, seeking me out of my darkness and bringing me back from this deep, black hole I had somehow fallen into. I felt myself looking deep into her grey eyes, and they bored into mine as if she was trying to read my mind. She knelt down in front of me, sitting on her knees as I crawled to lay my head on her lap, her tiny hands cradling my head. Her fingers delicately entwined themselves into my hair. I felt my heart slowly piecing itself together at her touch, as if she was healing my broken heart.

"I will always love you," she whispered to me before lifting my head slightly, so I sat up and faced her, her lips moving closer to mine. One small movement and we would be connected once again. I needed to feel her lips on mine. I moved myself closer, but every time I did, she moved farther away. Before I knew what was happening, her body was floating backwards away from me, I knelt back onto my shaky knees before pushing up onto my feet. My legs felt like weights. I looked down. I was barefoot and in ripped light jeans with my bare torso out. I couldn't work out what was going on, but I knew I needed to get to her. I needed to wrap my arms around her and pull her back down to me and never let go. I tried with every ounce of energy I had to make my legs move towards her. As I started to pick up my pace, she was getting higher and higher and farther out of reach. I screamed out her name. I couldn't lose her again. My fingertips just touched the flowing skirt of her dress, but I couldn't cling to her. Just as I was about to drop to my knees in defeat, I felt an almighty force pushing me back. My feet were taken off the floor, the air being ripped from my lungs in a blow. I gasped, desperately trying to catch my breath before being dropped into the calm ocean. I couldn't swim. The heavy weight was back, but this time it wasn't in my legs, it was in my chest, pushing me farther down to the sea bed. I couldn't scream. I couldn't do anything except let myself go. I closed my eyes, praying it was a dream and that I would wake up any moment.

My eyes sprung open when I felt her presence, her glow lighting up the dark sea I was slowly drowning in. Her wild auburn hair floated around her, her eyes on mine as I continued to sink. I smiled at her, knowing this would be the last time I saw her. A smile crept upon her face before she moved closer to me, her hands on my face, pulling me towards her as she kissed me with everything she had. My heart beat strongly in my chest as her tongue laced with mine, waking me from my current state. Then, as if she was magic, I felt like I could breathe again. I closed my eyes as I deepened the kiss, running my hands through her hair and never wanting to let go. I felt the warmth pumping around my body once more. Just as I was about to wrap my arms around her tiny waist, she was ripped away from me and I was forcefully launched upwards and out of the water. As soon as I broke the surface, the air hit my lungs, stinging at the brutal force. I looked down as I was suspended into the air, searching for her. I was so confused. I couldn't see her at all. I looked behind me, feeling a gust of wind coming from behind. As it passed me, I heard 'Carter' in a whisper, which broke me from this nightmare.

I jolted, gasping and searching round. It took me a moment to register that I was still lying on my kitchen floor, my phone still smashed, and still alone. I slowly sat up, catching my breath as I grasped at my chest, feeling my heartbeat punching in my chest. I was soaked, covered in sweat. Drips ran down my nose and I couldn't work out if they were tears or from my drenched hair. I gripped onto the worktop above me and slowly pulled myself up to grab a glass of water. After finishing it in two full mouthfuls, I shakily made my way upstairs. I needed to shower. I needed to wash away the nightmare.

It was just a nightmare.

CHAPTER FIVE

One Year Later

I sat back in my office chair after coming off a heated conference call with a new company I had recently bought. The old owner was a right ball ache, and I didn't have time for him today. I sat and reflected over the last year of my life while I had a breather. I never did hear from Freya. I still don't know whether that was her name flashing on my phone or not. It took me a while, but I had to accept it was over. I was still pining after her, still hoping I would get my chance and that fate would let us cross paths once more, but until then, I had to continue living my life. I would never be over her. How do you get over your one true love?

My phone buzzed. I looked over, always still hoping it would be her name, but it wasn't. It was Chloe's. Chloe was a woman I was seeing. It wasn't serious, but she helped fill a void. She wasn't like my Freya. She was the complete opposite, in fact. Not in her appearance, but in her personality. She was cold, calculated, stroppy, and spoiled. But she made me smile, and I needed to smile after my heartbreak. I had been seeing her for six months. She knew the deal. If I was to ever be graced with Freya's presence, I would always choose Freya. Always.

And she was okay with that. We worked. She didn't want serious, I didn't want serious. It just got us both through some tough times. I slid my thumb across and answered.

"Chloe." I smiled as I spoke.

"Hey. Still okay for dinner tonight?" she asked.

"Of course. Seven still work?"

"Yeah, that's fine. I've booked a table at Marco's."

I smiled again. She remembered I said I wanted to try out the new high-end Italian in the city.

"That's perfect. I can't wait. Thank you, Chloe."

"No problem. I'll see you soon. Miss your face," she cooed.

"I miss you too," I responded before cutting her off.

I placed my phone face down and sat back in my chair. I had a few moments before I went into the meeting. I just wanted to sit quietly for a moment. I literally just closed my eyes when my buzzer went on my office phone.

"Mr Cole, your two o'clock is here," Lilian said.

I leant forward and pressed the button. "No problem. I'll be there in five. Please get Wayne to offer drinks," I said with authority.

"Of course, Mr Cole," she said before cutting me off.

I linked my hands, turning my hands over and feeling the satisfactory crack of my fingers, then taking my arms and pushing them into the air and stretching out my spine. Sitting on those chairs was doing my back in. I huffed as I pushed myself away.

"Time to go," I muttered to myself before walking out of my office and into the meeting room. "Gentlemen," I greeted them before closing the heavy glass door.

***

I pulled my black suit trousers on, leaving them undone while I buttoned up the cuffs of my crisp white shirt. I stared at my physique in the mirror; I was finally getting my muscle tone back after letting myself go slightly. I felt good. I'd started to feel like myself again. I fastened the buttons to my shirt before tucking it into my trousers, doing up my trousers then slipping my feet into my black brogues. I walked into my bathroom, brushing my teeth then running wax through my hair, giving it my usual tousled look before spraying my Terre d'Hermès aftershave. I checked my watch; it was six thirty. Not sure why we had such an early reservation, but the earlier we ate, the earlier I could get home. No doubt Chloe would want to come home with me, but I would decide once we'd finished eating. I could do without it, to be honest. We had only slept together a couple of times. I tried to avoid it. Yeah, it was sex. But it just didn't feel right. I felt like I'd cheated on Freya, even though we weren't together. I just didn't have the connection with Chloe like I did with Freya. However, that was in the past, and that was where it needed to stay for the moment.

I walked back into the bedroom to put my phone in my pocket and pick my wallet off the dresser before I made my way downstairs. I smiled at Julia and wished her a good evening before she disappeared upstairs to her room while I waited for James to come and drive me to Chloe's.

She lived about ten minutes away from me, which made my life easier. It was twenty to seven by the time James came into the hallway.

"Sorry, Carter," he said as we walked towards the lift to the car park.

"No worries," I replied, sensing his tense mood.

We hardly spoke on the way to get Chloe which suited me. I would chat with him later if I was alone, make sure he was okay.

We pulled outside Chloe's and I called her.

"We're outside," I said, looking out the window up at her apartment block. I cut the phone off and placed it on my lap

"James." I leant forward to talk to him. "I just want to let you know I'm here if you want to vent. I don't want to pry, and I know I am technically your boss, but you are my friend and I care about you. If you want to talk, we can talk when I'm home."

34

"Thank you. That means a lot." His eyes focused on the front the whole time.

I jumped when I heard the car door open.

"Hey, baby," Chloe said in a silky voice before sliding in next to me. She was wearing a figure-hugging black gown with a slit up to her thigh, and high black stiletto heels. Her brown hair was swept to the side. She looked fantastic.

Before Freya, I would have thrown her down on the back seat and had my wicked way with her, but that just wasn't me anymore.

"You look wonderful." I beamed at her.

"Thank you. I feel wonderful," she said with lust in her eyes. I took her hand in mine and brushed it against my lips. She leaned into me and rested her head on my chest.

After a short ride, we arrived at the restaurant. As soon as we pulled up, James hopped out of the car and opened the door. I rolled my eyes as Chloe held her hand out for James to help her out of the car.

I felt my temper rise at her small action, but I let it slide. I didn't want to call her out and piss her off or annoy James.

Chloe stood on the pavement, smoothing down the silk gown over her curvy hips when I exited the car. As I stood up, I made sure my shirt was tucked in before placing my hand on James' shoulder and giving it a little squeeze, hoping he knew I was sorry for her actions. James was an employee, yes, but he doesn't get treated like that by anyone. I made a mental note to speak to her about it, delicately. She was so temperamental, she would lose her shit in the middle of the restaurant if I approached her in the wrong way and that wasn't what I needed in my life. I wanted an easy life.

"James, go home, clear your head. I'll get a taxi back."

"Carter, honestly…"

I cut him off by holding up my hand. "No, go home and chill. I am capable of a short taxi ride. It's not an ask, it's an order." I smiled at him as I started to walk away.

He bowed his head, accepting the order before he scuttled round to the front of the car and drove away.

I placed my hand on the base of Chloe's back, missing the familiar spark that coursed through me from Freya. I felt my heart start to crumble at the thought. A year on and I still missed her as if she had just left my life.

Chloe and I sat at the table and waited for our server to pour a bottle of red while we checked over the menu. As soon as the server walked away, Chloe's eyes glazed over, I could see the want in her eyes. She slowly ran her foot up my leg, trying to tease me. I knew where this evening was going. She wanted to be wined, dined then taken back to mine for more. I get frustrated with myself, as she is attractive, but the connection isn't there. I see her as more of a friend with benefits kind of girl, but I know she wants more, even though she knows Freya will always come above her.

"How about we do takeout and go home?" she said, lust lacing her voice.

"Easy tiger." I laughed, keeping my eyes on the menu.

"Let's eat out. I've wanted to come here since it opened."

"Fine. Let's just get something quickly then." She sat back, pouting her full lips.

She had already frustrated me with the way she treated James, and now she was sulking. I rolled my eyes and shook my head slightly at her brat-like behaviour. I felt like taking even longer now just to piss her off.

The server joined us, waiting for our order. Chloe scanned the menu again. "I'll take the truffle risotto, please," she said very sweetly.

The server nodded his head and jotted her order down. His eyes moved to mine. "I'll take the lobster ravioli, please," I said before shutting the menu and handing it back to him. He then took Chloe's from her.

As the server walked away, she sat forward, her elbows on the table, pushing her already full cleavage together. Her full red lips parted before she took her lip between her perfect white teeth. I would be lying if I said she didn't turn me on; I am a red-blooded male, after all. But each time I slept with her, I felt like a piece of me and Freya disappeared.

"Chloe, just a gentle reminder. James is my driver, and my friend. Don't treat him as your servant. I find it extremely disrespectful. I hope you understand," I said carefully, my eyes narrowing gently.

I let out a sigh of relief when I saw the server approach with our food. I was so hungry; I hadn't eaten since breakfast.

I groaned in appreciation as the ravioli hit my taste buds, and I smiled as Chloe made the same noise.

The food was stunning, but I was beat. I wanted to go home. I signalled the server over and asked for the bill. Chloe made it quite clear she was coming with me. It annoyed me that she didn't wait to be invited. I paid the bill then called for a taxi. I stood then walked behind Chloe and pulled her chair out. She smiled as she stood and clasped her hand over my wrist then ran her fingers slowly up my arm in a tantalizing manner. I knew where this night was going, and if I didn't give in, she wouldn't stop. I may as well just give her what she wanted.

It wasn't long before the taxi pulled up kerbside outside my penthouse. She was giving me her 'come fuck me' eyes as she stood outside the taxi with her hand on her hip. With her other hand, she was curling her finger for me to follow her. I let out a sigh before climbing out of the taxi and following her into the building.

We stepped into the lift, and I pushed the button, taking us to my penthouse. Just as the door closed, she pushed her lips onto mine, her hands in my hair as she kissed me fiercely. Her tongue went crazy, exploring my mouth. She was too desperate; her kiss was nothing on Freya's. Everything in me wanted to push her off, but I couldn't. I wouldn't. Freya didn't want me. I pushed Freya out of my mind as the lift doors opened.

Anger brewed within in me.

I broke away from Chloe, my lips burning from her forceful kiss. I grabbed her hand and pulled her down towards the bedroom, slamming the door behind me, ready to give her what she wanted. But it was far from what I wanted.

CHAPTER SIX

I was glad when Monday rolled round. After an unwanted weekend with Chloe, I was looking forward to getting away from her, as cruel as that sounded. She was too needy. She didn't give me any breathing space. I was so close to calling it off, but how could I? I didn't want to be an arsehole. I vowed after Freya that I wouldn't be that man again. The man before her. I walked into my office, sitting down at my desk and firing up my computer. I sat back in my chair, running my fingers down my pink tie when Laura appeared at my door, pulling me from my gaze.

"Laura," I said abruptly. We had hardly spoken since Freya. She still worked at You Magazine, but I had brought her over to Cole Enterprises to help out with some human resource issue we had.

"Carter," she said smoothly as she hung on the doorframe to my office. "Can I come in?"

"Do I have a choice?"

"Carter..." Her voice trailed off as she walked towards

me. "Don't be like that with me."

"How am I supposed to be? You won't talk to me about Freya. I have gone a year and not a single word from her!" I snapped, pushing my hand through my hair and pushing my mousy hair away from my forehead.

"She's stubborn," she said as she sat in front of my desk.

"No shit, Sherlock." Sarcasm laced my voice, which got an eye roll from Laura.

"Anyway, dipshit, I am here for a reason." She smirked at me as she leant back in her chair. "Freya called me this morning to ask whether you were going to the signing of Jude Priors in Paris. I checked your inbox to see you hadn't booked a flight, which I assumed means you're not going." Her eyebrows rose.

"That's right. I don't want to sign him. I would do it to piss Morgan off, but if it gives Freya a chance of a promotion and a new author signing, I couldn't take him away from her. I couldn't do that to her," I said quietly, my eyes flitting down to my clasped hands.

Morgan was my rival at Lornes & Hucks Publishing.

"Well, would you change your mind if I told you that she was going because you are not?" A smile creeps onto her face.

"She is?" I asked, surprised.

"Yup. Now, she would kill me if she knew I was here, talking to you about this. So, God, please. Do not tell her," she said, her eyes burning into mine in an intense stare.

41

"I won't." I nodded. I obviously would.

"Okay, so get booking your flight. She leaves on Friday with Morgan and Courtney." She stood from her seat.

"No worries. I'll be taking Chloe." The words were out before I realised what I'd said.

"Chloe?" she asked, an icy glare gracing her face. Shit, I forgot myself.

"Er, yeah. She's just a girl I'm seeing. It's nothing serious. She knows the deal. If I was to bump into Freya and she still wanted me then me and Chloe are over."

"Right. Well, let's just hope Freya does still want you." She smirked as she walked towards the door. Before she left, she turned on her heel. "Better get booking them flights, Cole." She smiled before walking away.

My heart was thumping.

Shit. This was it. My moment to get her back. Fuck.

I sat down at my desk, waking up the computer and typing in my password. I didn't give a shit about my work now. I needed to book my flights. I needed to sort out getting my soulmate back. I quickly typed in two tickets, but before I did, I called Chloe to check she actually wanted to come.

"Hey, it's me," I said.

"Hey, you."

"Fancy Paris this weekend? It's a work thing, but it's a nice break for the weekend."

"Oh my God, yes!" she screeched.

"Great. Pack a couple of ball gowns. There will be a dinner on Saturday night and we fly Friday and come home on Sunday," I said bluntly while I scanned through the flights.

"Okay, baby. I can't wait to spend the whole weekend with you."

"Mmhmm, bye." I cut her off before she could respond.

I called James to see if we could take the jet. The times were shocking, and I wanted to spend as much time in Paris as I could. He told me he would check and get back to me within the hour. Butterflies started dancing around in my stomach at the thought of seeing Freya. I started looking at hotels, then I realised I didn't know where she was staying.

I walked out of the office and headed up to human resources, my eyes scanning the office for Laura's blonde hair. I smiled when I saw her. I quickly walked over to her, bending down at her desk. "Hey, sorry to interrupt. Can you talk?" I asked.

"Someone's mood has improved," she said sarcastically.

"Oh, it has." I smirked at her. "Where is Freya staying?"

"Erm, let me check. She sent me an email. Give me five," she said as she started typing into her inbox. "Found it! Park Hyatt."

"Perfect. Thank you, Laura. Getting booked now. Thank you again," I said as I stood up and made my way back to my office.

I sat back in front of my computer and pulled up the hotel website. I didn't want to seem like a stalker, but I wanted to get as close to Freya as I could. I called the HR department. I didn't want to run there again. "Put me through to Laura, please." After a few rings, she answered. "What now, Cole?" She laughed.

"What room number is she in?"

"402, one of the presidential suites. Why?"

"Because I want to get as close to her as I can."

"Good luck." I could hear the smile in her voice.

I put the phone down and scrolled through the rooms. I found a suite on the same floor as Freya's. I couldn't choose a room though. I huffed as I dialled the hotel. After numerous departments and a translator, I finally booked a suite, room 406. Not as close as I wanted, but I was still close. My phone rang, it was James finally.

"James, good to take the jet?"

"Yes, all fine. When are you flying?" he asked.

"Friday. I want the earliest flight."

"Okay, give me a minute. I'll see what I can do." I sat waiting for him to come back on the line. A few minutes later, he came back. "Nine a.m. flight. That's the earliest I can get the jet out with air traffic control."

"That's fine. Get it sorted for me and Chloe."

"On it now, boss," James said before hanging up on me. I sat back in my desk and stretched up in my chair. This was my chance to get her back. My last chance.

***

Friday was soon upon us. We were up early and James was just about to drop us to the airport.

"You excited for our weekend away, baby?" Chloe asked as she stroked my arm.

"I am so fucking excited." If only she knew it wasn't because of her.

A small smile graced my face. I was so close to seeing Freya again. We exited the car, and James followed with the bags into the private lounge area of the airport while we waited to be called onto the plane. Chloe sat in the private bar, drinking a glass of champagne, while I had a glass of water and dealt with work emails. We were finally called onto the plane once my pilot, Richard, had the clearing from air traffic control.

We sat on the plane, and Chloe ordered a bottle of champagne for the journey. I was too nervous. I just wanted to close my eyes and land. And that's exactly what I did. I lost myself in a light sleep, my mind filled with pictures of my beautiful Freya.

A few hours later, we were at the hotel. I ushered her down the hallway quickly. I didn't want to risk being seen. I wanted to meet Freya on my terms, not by accident. Just as I was about to push open the door, Chloe stuck her tongue down my throat, offering me another night of her body. I pushed through the door quickly, slamming it behind me.

I pulled away from her, trying to catch my breath. "Calm it, woman," I huffed, agitated.

"You're no fun." She pouted as she sat on the bed.

"I'm tired, Chloe, and I have work to do." I shook my head as I disappeared into the lavish suite's bathroom.

I splashed my face with cold water before looking at myself in the mirror, watching the drips of water run down my nose and land in the sink. I was not having Chloe ruining this for me. If I ran into Freya, I wouldn't allow Chloe to fuck this up.

I needed to sit down and have the conversation with her. It was going to be hard, but she knew this day would come. I just didn't think I would ever get the chance to actually get this moment. I had played it out in my head every day since losing her. I wasn't about to let Chloe sabotage this. I patted my face with the hand towel then hung it back through the towel ring before making my way back into the room.

Chloe had started unpacking and hanging bits up in the large wardrobe space. She turned to me holding two ball gowns up; one navy, one black. "Which one shall I wear tomorrow night?" she asked, shaking her brown hair off her shoulders.

"Navy" I muttered, barely glancing in her direction.

"Gee, thanks for looking," she said sarcastically, screwing her face up.

"I did look. Hence why I chose navy!" I snapped back at

her.

"What's wrong with you? This isn't just tiredness, Carter. Don't bullshit me!" she shouted, throwing her ball gowns down on the bed.

I rolled my eyes at her tantrum. This was the time to tell her. Her response wasn't going to be good. I took a few moments to compose myself. I felt nervous. Not nervous of how she was going to react, but saying the words made it all very real all of a sudden.

"Freya is here," I said, getting straight to the point.

"Right," she replied, hands on her hips and attitude oozing out of her.

"You knew the deal, Chloe."

"She may not even want you. If she did, she wouldn't have left it so long. She would have called you," she hissed, a cruel smile spreading across her face.

"She may not. But I won't give up this time. So, as promised, I am giving you warning. If this does go the way I hope, we are finished. Do you understand?" I walked towards her, towering over her.

Her eyes went wide as she looked up at me. She pulled her full bottom lip between her teeth before slowly letting it go. "Gotcha."

"Good," I said with clear authority in my voice. "I mean it, Chloe. Don't fuck this up."

With that, she reached up and slapped me across the face. The noise was worse than the sting. My eyes glazed, my heart thumping as adrenaline started pumping through my body. "What the fuck was that for?" I hissed, moving even closer to her. I had never laid hands on a woman, and I never would, but she knew how to rile me up. She knew how to antagonize me.

"For fucking me about," she said as she pouted her lips. "You knew the deal," I spat.

"I did. But still, it felt good." She smirked before walking past me, running her fingertips over my shoulder before disappearing into the bathroom.

My blood was boiling. I wanted tomorrow night to be here. I needed to see Freya.

CHAPTER SEVEN

I sent Chloe out for the day on Saturday. I needed a few hours of peace. I had a shit ton of work to do and all she wanted was a day of sex. I didn't. So, I gave her my credit card and sent her shopping and to get her hair done. She liked being a kept woman; another thing I didn't particularly like anymore. Freya gave me many firsts, and because of that, I feared women were ruined for me. I honestly didn't feel anyone could live up to her.

I sounded pathetic, but I couldn't help it. I knew I loved her, I knew I wanted to be with her and only her, but the ball was in her court. I needed to win her back. I knew she hadn't stopped loving me, she was just too stubborn to admit she wanted me too.

I sat back in my chair, running my pen tip across my lips as my mind wandered to Freya. I thought about the last time we had sex at her mum and dad's house. She was so shy when I first met her, but I loved that I managed to bring her out of her shell a bit. The way she bounced up and down on my cock, her full tits bouncing up and down. My hands holding onto her hips, her body curvaceous in all the right places. I felt the tightness around my jeans as my cock grew hard thinking about her. All I wanted at that moment was to sink myself into her. I undid my jeans buttons and pulled them down slightly before relieving my aching cock from my boxers. I wrapped my hand around myself and started thinking about her again while rubbing my hand up and down my thick shaft fast. It didn't take long until I orgasmed hard, pushing my cock back into my boxers and letting my arousal soak into them. I stood from the desk and walked into the bathroom, stripping off and stepping under the hot shower.

God, I hoped I could sort this out. I needed to be with her.

A few hours had passed, and Chloe bounded through the door at five like an excited puppy. I smiled up at her as I took in her appearance. Her long brown hair had been curled and clipped away from her face. Her make-up was a lot heavier than usual, and her lips were matte red. "You look nice," I said as she walked towards me, planting a kiss on my cheek.

"You okay?" she asked as she started peeling her clothes off and walking towards the bathroom.

"I am. You?"

"Perfect." She smiled as she closed the door behind her. I pulled my navy suit out of the wardrobe and laid it on the bed. I showered earlier so I just needed to put my deodorant on and do my hair. I debated shaving, but I was digging the slight stubble I had grown. It wasn't a full-on beard, but I was definitely sporting a five o'clock shadow. I rubbed my hand over it before grabbing my white shirt and navy bow tie.

Chloe opened the bathroom door and was wearing just a white lacy underwear set. She walked over to me seductively before pressing her palms on to my chest.

"Fuck me," she whispered in my ear before tracing soft kisses down my jawline.

"No," I replied, grabbing her hands and pulling them away from me. Her eyes shot up at me, a frown forming on her forehead as she pulled her brows together. "Not tonight." I walked away from her, starting to undress.

"This is because of her, isn't it?"

"Chloe, not now, for fuck's sake. We need to be out of here at six thirty."

"You're an arsehole." She shook her head as she grabbed her navy gown, hanging it up.

"Never claimed not to be, sweetheart." I chuckled as I pulled my t-shirt over my head.

She stormed back into the bathroom in a huff then slammed the door behind her.

I shook my head at her. She was such a child. I folded

my jeans and t-shirt up and left them on the bed before slipping into my fitted skinny suit trousers and shrugging my tight white shirt up my arms. I tucked myself in before doing the buttons up then running my bowtie under my collar. Once satisfied that it was all under, I folded my collar back down and tied my bowtie. I put my suit jacket on then styled my hair with wax before spraying a good amount of Terre D'Hermes aftershave. I slipped my Rolex onto my wrist then sat on the bed to slip my tanned Oxfords on.

I was getting agitated waiting for Chloe. She didn't have to shower or do her hair, so what the fuck was she doing? I stood up and knocked on the bathroom door.

"Hurry up. We've got to go," I said before sitting back on the bed.

A few minutes later, she appeared, still in her underwear and looking no different. God knows what she was doing. Well, I do know. She was winding me up. I would not rise to her. She sat down next to me before slipping her silver heeled sandals on, then sashayed her way over to the wardrobe and picked her navy floor-length gown off the hanger. I watched as she let it pool at her feet before stepping into it effortlessly and pulling it up to her chest.

"Do me up," she said bluntly.

I stood and grabbed the zipper, pulling it up and then clasping the dress together at the top. "Done," I said before sitting back on the bed. I must admit, she looked wonderful. She had a smaller frame than Freya, but she was still curvy.

Her hips and thighs were thicker than Freya's, but it suited her. I eyed the slit that sat on her thigh. "Not a bit too much?" I asked, shrugging as I stood up.

"No, not at all." She shrugged back at me before applying more matte lipstick.

I walked over to her then kissed her on the cheek. "You ready?" I asked.

"Yup." She sighed as she clasped my hand. "You know, if you change your mind and decide that you don't feel what you did for Freya, I'll still be here, okay? I love you, Carter," she said quietly as we walked into the hallway.

"I know," I replied before pulling our suite door closed.

We jumped in a taxi outside and made our way to the restaurant. The roads were busy, and I started to worry we would be too late and turned away at the door. It was bad enough that I RSVP'd late to the signing. I really didn't see the point of this dinner, and if I was here for the actual signing and not Freya then there was no way I would be coming to this stuffy, uptight dinner with potential rival companies. It was bad enough that Morgan was going to be there. I despised the man. God knows why Freya agreed to work there. The bloke knew nothing when it came to publishing and running a successful business.

After thirty minutes of stop/start traffic in the hustle and bustle of Paris, we finally arrived at the restaurant. My heart felt like it was going to explode from behind my ribs I was so nervous. I gave the driver his cash and made my way up to the restaurant door. The doorman stopped us and asked for our names, his eyes running down the list in his hand.

"Carter and Chloe, CHP Publishing," I said quickly. He trailed down the list and onto the second page, shaking his head before looking at the first page again. "Aha. Sorry, your name was crossed out and re-written again. My bad," he said apologetically, his thick French accent present.

"Not a problem," I said, walking past him.

"Second door on your right," he shouted after me as we walked into the grand lobby then made our way into the dining room.

I was annoyed that we were right over the back of the room. I couldn't see the entrance doors from where I was sitting, but I knew Freya would be here soon. I pulled Chloe's chair out for her, then tucked her in before I pulled out my own seat. I took my jacket off and hung it onto the back of my chair while slowly scanning the room for Freya, but I couldn't see her. A young waitress approached us and asked for our drink order. I ordered us a bottle of white and two tap waters then dismissed her.

I looked around the table. We were sitting with an older team from Germany who were there to try and get Jude. Didn't seem like his bag, but I could be surprised tomorrow when news hit on who he signed to. Lornes and Hucks did have a good chance, as much as that annoyed me. If I wasn't so desperate to get Freya back, I would have made a play for him as well. He was such a talented writer and would do wonders for whatever publishing house was lucky enough to get him.

I was grateful when the waitress came over. Chloe had her hand on my thigh, squeezing it regularly as if she was trying to show people her claim to me. I thanked the waitress as she poured our glasses then put the wine into a chiller on the table before walking away.

I felt the air shift. I knew she was there.

The hairs on the back of my neck stood, goosebumps covering my skin. I turned in my chair, my eyes once again scanning the room. Still nothing. I sighed in frustration. I shrugged it off and tried to focus on the here and now. I knew she was going to be there. I was told by Laura. Holy fuck. What if she played me? What if she knew Freya wasn't going to be there and she only said it to get me away from her? I shook the thought away as I was brought back into the room when dinner was served, I was grateful for the distraction for a few moments.

Once dinner was cleared, Chloe excused herself to go to the bathroom, but not before kissing me on the lips passionately, clearly trying to claim what was hers, but that was the problem – I wasn't hers. I sat back in my chair and relaxed slightly. I was sick of wearing my bow tie. I wanted to rip it off, but I couldn't. The rest of the table was engaged in light chatter. I just sat back, observing them with a stony glare. My phone beeped, my heart racing at the thought that it could be Freya. But no, of course it wasn't. It was James.

Hey boss, how's it going? Have you been reunited with Freya yet? J

I let out a snort before tapping a quick response.

No such luck mate. I can feel her here, I just can't see her. The room is fucking huge and we have been sat right at the back. But, the evening isn't over. I'm not giving up. Thank for checking in. I hope you're okay? C

Within minutes, he replied.

I have faith boss. You two are made for each other. And yes, not bad. See you Sunday. Planes all booked for an afternoon flight. Will text details on Sunday. J

I smiled at his message before putting my phone back in my suit pocket when I felt a hand run across my shoulder. I looked up to see Chloe beaming at me then taking her seat next to me and flashing me her smile. I turned slightly and smiled back at her. She wrapped her arms around me, pulling me into an embrace as she whispered in my ear that she wanted me to take her home. I ignored her and pulled away then turned to signal the waiter for a whisky. That was when I felt it, her presence. Her eyes on me. I looked straight ahead of me and saw her standing there, champagne in hand. Her mouth dropped open. My sage eyes found hers. Fuck. She was there.

CHAPTER EIGHT

I didn't hesitate. I was up like a shot as I made my way towards her. I could see her eyes searching for Courtney, no doubt to rescue her, but she wasn't getting away that easily. I was finally face to face with her. Her scent intoxicated me.

Fuck, I can't believe she's here.

"Hello, Freya," I said, apprehension lacing my voice, my eyes flitting back and forth to hers.

"Hey," she said in a small, timid voice.

Fuck. Even her voice made me hard. I had to keep my cool. I needed to play it down. I saw her look past me and focus on Chloe.

"Erm, your date is waiting for you." She nodded towards the table. I turned and looked over my shoulder to see Chloe with a disgusted look on her face, her eyes boring into me and Freya.

I let out my held breath. "Don't worry about her for the minute. She can wait," I said abruptly as I looked over my shoulder again, giving Chloe a warning glance. As I turned back to face Freya, I saw she was about to walk away.

"Okay, so I'm going to go back to my table." Her eyes searched for Courtney again, then she looked down at her hands and knotted her fingers. I smirked. She was nervous. She always knotted her fingers when she was nervous.

"No you don't." I continued to smirk. "Follow me outside. I want to talk to you." My smile widened and spread across my face. I brushed past her and walked into the lobby area of the restaurant. As our shoulders touched, I felt that electric spark course through me. I'd missed the feeling she brought me. She had bought me back from the never-ending darkness I had been living in for the last year. I worried she wasn't going to follow, but within seconds, I heard her heels on the tiled floor. I breathed in the fresh air, filling my lungs as I waited for her to come closer to me. As soon as I felt she was there, I couldn't help but slowly undress her with my eyes. She looked fucking breath-taking. Her tanned, long legs disappeared into a black dress, and I had to contain myself from throwing her down on the floor and tasting and exploring every fucking inch of her perfect body.

"Freya, as always, you look beautiful." I loved that I could still make her blush.

"You look nice too." She smirked at me, but within seconds, she had recomposed herself. "What do you want, Carter?"

"Oh, I love it when you're mad." I grinned down at her then taking a step closer to her.

"I'm not mad. I'm cold." She moaned as she crossed her arms across her chest then looked down at the floor. I could see the pain I'd caused on her face; she wasn't even trying to hide the heartbreak. This was all because of me. I destroyed her.

It took me a moment to speak.

"I just wanted to see how you are. We haven't spoken in a year, and, well, I didn't know if I would get this opportunity," I said, running my hand round the back of my head and looking down at my feet. I felt her eyes burning into me. I slowly lifted my face up, grinning as her eyes met mine.

"I'm okay. Being kept busy at work, which is good." She nodded. "What about you? You seem happy."

Oh, darling, you couldn't be further from the truth. I was a broken man who didn't think I could be fixed again. I didn't think I would get this chance to be with the one I loved again. She carried on, "I bumped into your girlfriend in the toilet. A bit full of herself, but I wouldn't expect anything less. That's what I meant when I said I couldn't be what you wanted. Her. That's not me." She finally took a breath.

She went to speak again, but I silenced her by putting my index finger over her plump lips. "Shh." I wrapped my arm around her and pulled her close to me. "For starters," I said, "She isn't my girlfriend, she is my date. Secondly, I didn't want you to be like her. I wanted you to be like you." I slowly ran my fingers across her lip then started trailing it down her chin and then across her jawline. Her breath caught. She was still clearly affected by me, like I was with her. "I've missed you, Freya. More than you could ever know. I had no choice but to let go seeing as Miss Stubborn didn't have the decency to return any of my calls." She went to talk, but I stopped her. "But enough about that. Let's not dwell on the past."

Nothing else was said in that moment, we just stared at each other in silence, neither of us quite sure what to say.

She placed her hands on my chest, and just that one bit of contact brought my soul back to life. It reignited something deep inside of me. She bowed her head and closed her eyes. I tightened my arms around her, my breathing starting to calm. I didn't want to move, I wanted to stay with my arms wrapped around her for as long as I possibly could.

I felt my phone ringing, and Freya pulling away from me. I sighed deeply as I dropped my arms and let her go. I watched as she moved away from me and wrapped her arms around herself to keep warm. I stepped back to speak to Chloe.

I walked towards her, feeling even more agitated now than I did earlier. "That was Chloe."

"Oh, is that your date?" Freya asked.

"Yup," I said bluntly as I straightened my bow tie. I didn't think when my next question slipped out. "Can I see you tomorrow? We're staying in the same hotel."

I watched as her eyes widened. "Oh my God, it *was*

you!"

"What? When did you see me?"

Bollocks. How did she see me?

"Last night, me and Courtney were going into our room and I saw you go into your room with your tongue down someone's throat, which I am now assuming was Chloe," she said bitterly, as if her name was poison on her tongue.

Typical she saw us at that moment when Chloe shoved her tongue into my mouth. I didn't even bloody want her. Oh, my darling Freya. Why did she have to see that?

"I can't meet you tomorrow. Are you deluded?" I could see she was trying to stop herself from getting upset and I felt like she was breaking my heart all over again. "Carter, do you not understand how much you hurt me? You can't just pick me up, especially now you're with someone new!" Her voice grew louder. Passers-by were staring at us, but I didn't care, and neither did she. "I shouldn't have come out here with you. What was I thinking?" She shook her head, laughing at herself. "Bye, Carter. Enjoy your trip," she snapped before turning to walk away.

I pulled her back round to face me. I didn't give her a chance to get away again. I wrapped my arms around her and picked her up, my mouth finding hers. I let out a moan as my tongue caressed hers softly, waiting for the green light. Her tongue danced with mine as our kiss became fiercer. We were kissing as if we were each other's last breath of air on the planet.

A low, soft moan left her as we lost ourselves in each other. I placed her down; I needed to compose myself. I was so fucking horny. I ran my hand up to her beautiful face and slowed my kiss down as my lips connected with hers again. She pulled away, biting her lip, blushing from head to toe.

"Freya, fuck. God, I've missed you" I stammered. My heart was pumping so fast I was scared it was going to explode with the returning feelings that plagued my body.

"I've missed you too." I watched as she touched her lips, reliving the moment I kissed her mere moments ago. I walked back to her, kissing her once more, this time softly and more tentatively.

She pulled away from me but my heart was still racing. I took her hand and rubbed my finger across her knuckles. We stood quietly for a moment. There was so much I still wanted to say, but I didn't want to forget this moment. The moment I saw her again after this year of hell. Her auburn hair was pulled away from her face, and the lower part of her hair was curled and tumbling down her back. Her big, grey eyes stayed on mine the whole time, her plump lips red from the rush of blood from my kiss. Her short black dress clung to her perfect body.

"You'd better get back to Chloe. She's going to wonder where you are," she said bitterly, pulling her hand from mine quickly and lowering her eyes down to her shoes. "Enjoy your evening. Goodnight, Carter."

"No, please don't..." But it was useless. She couldn't

63

hear me. Before I could stop her and grab her once more, she ran towards the stairs and into the restaurant. I was left watching her walk away from me. I felt empty and hollow.

I will do everything in my power to get her back. I'll make sure of it.

I ran into the ballroom, running my hands through my hair and pushing it back off my face slightly. I walked along the side of the room so I didn't need to pass directly past her table.

I just wanted to go back to her.

I sat down at the table when Chloe started questioning me. "Where the fuck have you been?" she hissed, still keeping a smile plastered on her face to save drawing attention to us from our table guests.

"With Freya," I said bluntly, kissing her on the cheek.

I felt nothing. The fire was still burning in my soul for Freya. I was besotted and obsessed with her. I turned to face her table; she was chatting to Courtney and I could see the sheer pain I had caused her embedded on her face. Her beautiful face. She grabbed her bag and ran out of the restaurant.

I couldn't let her go again.

I pushed myself away from the table, walking quickly to get to the lobby. My heart raced when I saw her still standing there, her back to me.

She turned to face me.

"Freya, please," I said, letting out a sigh. "Meet me tomorrow. I need to see you again."

"I can't do this again, Carter. I can't get hurt again. I'm still not over the last time." Her eyes glassed over.

"Freya, I never want to hurt you again. Please, just meet me tomorrow."

Her lips parted as she went to talk before the cretin Courtney barged into me, pushing past me to get to Freya.

"Come on, hun. Let's go back to the hotel." She started dragging Freya away before turning back to me, her long blonde hair swishing in her face as she did. "You are not doing this to her again. Not on my watch." Then she marched herself and Freya out of the restaurant.

I must admit, as much as I didn't like the pest that she was, I couldn't deny how much she cared for Freya.

I took five deep breaths, trying to calm myself. When Freya first left me, I saw a therapist. I needed to burden someone else with the shit in my life other than myself. She taught me to breathe before I reacted. After five deep breaths, I ran for the door. I needed to stop her, but I was too late. I stood in the road, watching Freya drive away, looking at me as she disappeared into the distance.

Last time it was me driving away from her, and her standing there. Now it was the other way around.

I threw my head back, pissed off with myself and the

situation. I was bought back to reality when a taxi sounded its horn to warn me. I told them to go fuck themselves before walking back into the restaurant, defeated.

I was livid; I could feel my blood boiling. As I went to enter the restaurant, I was greeted by Morgan. Brilliant. Just what I needed.

"Ah, Carter. Get away, did she?" he taunted me.

"Fuck off, Morgan!" I snapped.

"Don't worry, big man. I'm sure you will get her eventually," he said sarcastically, laughing as he walked towards the front entrance.

I growled as I made my way through the hustle and bustle and saw Chloe walking towards me. *Here we go*.

"You're an embarrassment!" she snapped.

"Not as much as you" I said with aggression in my voice. Nasty Carter was coming out. All my anger from my youth was rearing its ugly head and I couldn't tame it.

"Uncalled for."

"It's the truth. I am done. Stay the night, but I want you gone in the fucking morning. You have never, and will never be any more than a pity fuck!" I spat.

"You're an arsehole," she said before storming away.

"Yes, I am." I smiled as I watched her walk away.

I went to the bar in the ballroom and ordered a straight whisky on ice. I needed something to cool the rage brewing deep in my body. I grabbed the tumbler and threw it back.

"One more," I said.

I needed something to calm me down, to calm me before I claimed Freya as my own once more.

CHAPTER NINE

As I sat in the taxi back to the hotel, I tried calling Freya again and again, but no response. Of course not. Miss Stubborn was back with force. I ran through the hotel and into my suite. I went straight into the bathroom, ignoring Chloe completely. I splashed my face with some water, calming my breathing before I went to her room. I re-styled my hair and exited the bathroom then the suite, slamming the door behind me.

I stood outside her room, 402. I stared at the number on the door for a few moments before banging on the door loudly. No answer. I banged again. Maybe she wasn't staying here. Maybe she had switched rooms. I placed both hands on the door frame, bowing my head, defeated. I was about to give up when I heard stamping footsteps coming towards me.

"Courtney, why didn't you take your key?" Freya groaned, swinging the door open. Her hand clung onto the suite door. "Oh."

I couldn't keep my eyes off her. Her hair was now completely down and tousled. She was wearing a black silk nightdress with lace detail around her breasts. She was fucking breath-taking.

"Carter, please go. I'm tired. I can't do this tonight."

"No chance," I whispered back as a wicked grin spread across my face, I pushed myself off the door frame, shutting the door behind me. I placed my hands either side of her face, studying every single detail. "Freya," I whispered. Her name sounded so good on my tongue. I touched her lips softly, kissing her. I pulled away from her, looking deep into her eyes. I felt like I was looking into her soul. Her hands slowly moved into my hair, and all my tension washed away at her touch. She pulled me towards her, kissing me, her tongue slowly finding mine, massaging it seductively. I ran my hands down her body, feeling the thin silk over her curves stopping at her hips. I squeezed slightly as our kiss got deeper and fiercer, all of our heartbreak and emotion consuming that one kiss. She was my oxygen. I needed her like the air I breathed. She was my reason for existence, my reason for survival.

I snaked my arms around her waist while still lost in her. While kissing, I picked her up. Her legs wrapped round me as I walked her over to the bed, dropping her down gently. Pulling away, I looked down at her. She was glowing, her eyes shining.

I leant down and rested my forehead on hers. "I really have missed you," I mumbled.

"I've missed you more," she whispered.

I leant down and met my lips with hers, taking her again. I kissed her softly. I wanted to remember every single detail of tonight.

She moved back towards the headboard, pulling me towards her. I pushed her legs apart and kneeled in between them. I couldn't keep my eyes off her and how stunning she looked. I ran my hands up the silkiness of her nightie.

"I need to get this off you," I said in a low growl.

I slowly came to her face to face, smiling, keeping my eyes on hers the whole time. I slid my hand up her thigh, memorizing every detail of her skin. I slowly pushed her silk nightdress up with my hand. I smirked when her breath caught at my touch; she still responded like before. I brushed my fingertips over her lacy black knickers. I had to control myself. She moaned at my gentle touch, and I gently caressed her sweet spot through her knickers. She pushed my hand away, her breathing fast. I lowered myself over her, planting soft kisses along her jawline, slowly moving down to her neck then moved on to her collarbone.

I tugged at her nightdress and released her perfect breasts. I took one straight into my mouth, sucking and licking as she moaned in response to my touch. I moved to her other one, doing the same, sucking and licking. I then blew on her nipples, which caused a small whimper from

her.

I slid my free hand down her body and laced my fingers in her underwear before pulling them to the side. I brushed the tips of my fingers across her sweet spot once more, not pulling my tongue from her hard nipples.

"Carter," she moaned. "Please."

I smirked against her skin. "Shh. I'm not ready to stop yet." I grinned up at her again.

My fingers slowly found her sweetness, and I slid them in slowly, deep into her.

She moaned out loud, her back arching. I carried on sucking and licking her nipples while slowly plunging my fingers into her soaked core, my thumb brushing against her sensitive bud. She was so wet. I found her eyes on me, watching what I was doing.

Her breath hitched and she started panting as her orgasm was impending. I could feel her clamping tightly around my fingers. With one last stroke, and a flick of my tongue against her now over-sensitive nipples, she came crashing down around me, moaning out loud as she scrunched the bed sheets with her hands. I pulled my fingers from her, placing them on my lips and pushing them into my mouth, sucking her sweet arousal off my fingers.

"Just like I remember. So sweet." She turned a crimson red, throwing her arm over her face, embarrassed by my crude outburst. "Don't be shy. We're only just getting started. We have a lot of making up to do." I grinned down at her.

I couldn't get over how stunning she was, and how lucky I was that I was back with her at that moment. I forgot about everything and just took this moment to enjoy what we had, right here, right now.

She sat up slowly, reaching out and putting her hands on my chest. She started undoing the buttons of my white shirt. I watched as her eyes marvelled at my body. Her greedy hands were on my suit trousers as she undid the button and tugged them down. She ran her hands up my body. Her eyes watched where her fingers touched as if she was trying to memorize every inch of me. She leant up and pushed my shirt off my shoulders, watching it drop to the floor. I pulled back and stood, pushing my trousers down to my ankles and kicking them off. I smirked as she sat back, perching on her elbows and admiring the view. Little minx.

I grabbed the top of her thighs and pushed them apart. I lowered myself back in between her legs and covered her soaked core with my mouth, my tongue flicking and teasing her.

I grew hard instantly. My boxers felt tight over my growing bulge. I pushed my hands up around her hips and tightened my grip. I continued to caress every inch of her sweet spot, her pelvis moving as she started to climb once more. I stopped, kneeling up and making my way to her lips, hungrily kissing her mouth, I wanted her to taste just how sweet she was. My wandering hands grabbed the hem of her nightdress, breaking our kiss before pulling it over her head, marvelling at the sight in front of me. My gorgeous Freya sitting there in just her black lacy knickers. She was a sight for sore eyes. She was fucking stunning.

I inhaled sharply as I admired her. She stood up, turning towards me and pushing me down onto the bed, placing her legs either side of me as she straddled me. I placed my hands around her waist and pulled her down towards me, our mouths finding each other once more. She moaned as my tongue teased hers, our kiss getting deeper as we started to lose ourselves in each other. Her hands were back in my hair, gently tugging and pulling. I slowly pushed her up off me while I pulled my boxers down. I wanted her to ride my cock until it was dry. I tucked my fingers in the side of her knickers and pulled them down. She slipped them down and then flicked them off her ankle.

This was it, the moment I claimed her as mine once more, and I would never let her out of my grip again.

I held onto her hips as she lowered herself down onto me. I had to stop my eyes rolling in the back of my head on contact as I stretched her tightness once more. She let out a gasp as she took every inch of me. She moved her hips slowly on top of me, letting out sweet moans.

I mirrored her slow, torturous movements. I ran my hand round the back of her head, pulling her down to my mouth as our lips met again, our tongues entwining. She continued to thrust her hips back and forth. My breathing started to get heavier; the sensation was overwhelming. She pulled away from me, sitting back up then looking down at me, her grey eyes hazy with lust.

She was turned on, turned on at the fact that she had me underneath her.

I placed my other hand back on her hip as I moved with her again, this time hitting her deeper than before. She started tightening around me again. I knew she was going to come undone soon.

"Come for me, Freya," I moaned out. "You are such a turn on."

I groaned as I continued to thrust my hips harder into her. She started moving faster as she met my thrusts.

"Shit, Freya," I growled through gritted teeth.

She threw her head back as she continued to move on me, her hips pursuing the sweet movements that were about to make us both combust with pleasure. I tightened my grip on her hips and she moaned loudly as she came hard. I slammed up into her once more before finding my own release, moaning her name as I came down from heaven.

"Freya, what do you do to me?" I sat up and cradled her, wrapping my arms tightly around her and kissing her once more. Our bodies were hot and sweaty. We were completely lost in each other.

We laid in silence next to each other, still naked. I wanted to say so much, but I didn't want to ruin this moment for either of us. I didn't know if this meant we were back together or not. I didn't want to ask at that moment.

Freya rolled over and pulled the duvet up to her chest, clutching it tightly before closing her eyes. I wrapped my arms around her, pulling her into me as I nuzzled my face into her neck, letting out a deep sigh before breathing in her luscious scent.

I pressed my soft lips against her neck, trailing them along to her jawline. She moved slowly to face me as she found my lips. "I've missed lying with you," I whispered before kissing her earlobe.

"I've missed you too" she whispered back. She clasped my hand, squeezing it. "We are so wrong for doing this." She rolled over to face me so she was lying on her side. "I'm just as bad as Jake and Aimee." She scowled and bowed her head.

I was annoyed that she would even think that.

I put my hand under her chin and lifted her face up to look at me, her grey eyes full of doubt. "You are nothing like them."

She didn't say any more, just stared at me as if she was trying to focus on every inch of my face. I lay on my side, propping myself up on my elbow, moving my free hand up and placing it on the side of her face, slowly rubbing her cheek with the pad of my thumb. I wanted to lie here all night, never having to leave her again.

As If she read my mind, she said, "You'd better go." She rolled onto her back. "It's early hours and Chloe will wonder where you are. Plus, I have a big day tomorrow and I really do need to sleep."

I huffed, placing my hand on her belly. "But I don't want to go," I said, furrowing my brow.

"I don't want you to go, but you're not mine to keep." She smiled weakly at me, shattering my heart. I had truly broken her.

"I've always been yours."

"Let's not get into this now. As it stands, you're with Chloe. You brought her here with you."

She was right; I did bring her with me, but only because I didn't know whether Freya wanted to see me, or even be here for that matter.

"Don't go to see Jude tomorrow. Stay in bed with me," I said, giving her my smouldering eyes.

She responded by nudging me with her elbow. "I have to go. It's the whole reason Morgan brought me here. Same reason you're here. To nab Jude from us." She sat up with the bed sheet still clinging to her glistening body.

"I didn't come here for Jude," I said bluntly "I came here for you."

She turned her head slightly to look at me, doubt all across her face.

"Why are you lying? If you came here for me, you wouldn't have come with her. Don't bullshit me, Carter," she said bitterly, shaking her head before leaving the bed, dropping the sheet and walking round to the foot of it.

"Please, Freya. I'm not bullshitting you." I sat up in the bed and sighed, my eyes burning into hers.

"Well, I'm here, but it doesn't change anything. You're with her. Can you just go, please?" she said with venom clear in her voice.

I was pissed off that she doubted me, and pissed off that she kept throwing Chloe in my face, but could I blame her? No, I couldn't.

"Fine. If that's what you want. I'm not going to Jude's signing tomorrow. I will be in my room. Chloe is going home tomorrow morning. The offer is still there to spend the day with me."

I slid off the bed with the bed sheet clinging to my waist, bending down to pick my boxers up then dropping the sheet and giving her the perfect view of my arse. I looked over my shoulder, knowing full well she wouldn't be able to not look and winked at her, grinning. I pulled my boxers and trousers up in one swift move and shrugged my shirt on, leaving the buttons undone.

I walked over to her, tilting her chin with my thumb and finger, kissing her delicately. "I don't want to lose you again, Freya."

She smiled but looked down at her feet. I didn't move, her eyes drifting back up to mine. She was trying to keep it together. I could see her throat bobbing as if she was trying to swallow down the lump that was evident.

"How can you lose something you never had?" she said quietly.

I didn't know what to say. She was right. I tucked a strand of her auburn hair behind her ear and kissed her once more, this time lingering then walking towards the door.

"You know where I will be tomorrow. Just me and you. Think about it," I said, looking over my shoulder at her one last time before leaving. I stood on the other side of the suite door in the hallway, sliding down it and throwing my head in my hands.

Fuck.

CHAPTER TEN

I walked quietly into the suite. Chloe was tucked in the massive queen-sized bed. I shrugged my shirt off and folded my trousers up before pulling the throw off of the bed and laying it over me on the sofa that was tucked under the window. I didn't want to sleep next to Chloe, especially after spending the night with Freya.

I shouldn't have brought Chloe. I honestly didn't even know why I did. I didn't think. Now I have to deal with her in the morning. She is going to be pissed. She was pissed off last night, and the fact that I left her here on her own to be with Freya is going to agitate her even more. I tried not to think about it anymore. I looked at my phone, debating whether to text Freya. I decided the latter. I couldn't force her to spend the day with me, I could only hope. I closed my eyes and tried to quiet my mind so I could sleep. I needed to sleep.

I was awoken mere hours later by the feeling of someone watching me. I forced my eyes open to see Chloe standing over me, wearing a lounge suit, clearly fucked off.

"Spend the night with that slut, did you?" she hissed before pulling the throw off me, revealing my bare chest and boxers.

"Chloe, leave it," I growled as I slowly sat up and rubbed my eyes.

"So you did then." She crossed her arms over her chest.

"Yes."

"You're a bastard." She slapped my cheek hard as she stormed into the bathroom. My cheek instantly stung; I was livid.

I shot up and ran for the bathroom door, banging on it hard with my fist. "Chloe! Open the fucking door, now!" I continued to bang.

"Go away!"

I ran my hand through my hair, pushing it back away from my face and sat on the bed, my fingers laced in between each other, my elbows resting on my legs as I started to shake them to keep my mind busy. I started doing the breathing exercises my therapist showed me. Inhale deeply through the nose, exhale slowly through the mouth. I was meant to do it five times, but on the second exhale, Chloe opened the door so hard I thought she was going to rip it off the hinges.

"Do I mean nothing to you?" she asked. She had clearly been crying.

"Chloe, I do like you. But I could never love you." I sighed, too tired to argue.

"Why?" she asked quietly.

"Because it's only Freya. It's always only been her." She didn't say anything, she just sat next to me. "You knew this. You knew the deal before we got into this." I turned to face her. Her eyes were on her hands which were in her lap. "You knew if I ever got the chance, I would always choose her."

"You're such a prick!" she shouted at me again as she stood up and started pulling her clothes out of the wardrobe.

"I think it's best you go home. I can get you onto a flight within the hour," I said.

"I don't want your help. I'm going anyway."

I left her to it. We could go on like this all day.

I walked into the bathroom and let the hot water run over me, washing everything from this morning away. I wrapped the towel around my waist and walked into the bathroom to find Chloe lying on the bed, stark bollock naked.

"What the fuck are you doing?" I asked, clinging onto the towel. "That's not happening." I half-laughed as I reached for my bag to get some clean boxers. I sat on the bed next to her, not even looking at her as I undid my towel and slid my boxers up my legs.

Just as I went to stand, she climbed onto my lap, wrapping her arms around my neck, trying to kiss me.

"Chloe, get off me, please." I pried her arms from round my neck. I could feel how soaked she was through my boxers.

I stood up with her legs wrapped round me and dropped her to the bed before covering her up with my towel.

"Get dressed. I've got to go down to reception. I want you gone by the time I get back, okay?" I asked her as I pulled a pair of grey cuffed jogging bottoms up my legs and then a white t-shirt over my head.

"Bye, Chloe," I muttered as I got to the suite door. She nodded. She couldn't even look at me. I shut the door behind me and made my way to reception.

I said goodbye to the receptionist and jumped in the lift. I was glad Chloe had gone. There was no reason for her to stay; she had embarrassed herself. She knew this was the deal. She was some kind of therapy for me when I lost Freya, and she was there for me in ways no one else could be. I would be forever grateful to her, but she wasn't Freya. I loved Freya and only wanted to be with her. No one could ever stand up to how much that woman meant to me.

I took a deep breath as the lift pinged to signal I was at my floor when I heard a horrendous scream.

"Get off me, you psycho!" Freya screamed.

Dear God. Chloe was lashing around and hitting Freya. I ran down the corridor.

"Chloe!" I shouted. "Get the fuck off her!" I ran up behind Chloe and grabbed her round the waist, dragging her off Freya. She was screaming and clawing my hands like some possessed demon. I continued to drag her into the room and slammed the door behind me. I just wanted to go out to Freya, make sure she was okay, but I had to deal with Chloe first.

"What the fuck do you think you're doing?" I shouted at her.

"She's a whore, a homewrecker!" she snapped back at me, touching up her smudged lipstick then attending to her messy hair.

"She is none of those things. You agreed. You knew the deal, Chloe!" I slammed my fist down on the table, anger rising from the pit of my stomach. No breathing exercises could bring me back down. "Get up, get your bag, and GET THE FUCK OUT!"

She stomped over to her bag and made her way to the door. I didn't give her a chance to say anything. I grabbed her arm firmly, opening the door for her and frog marching her down to the lift. I pressed the button numerous times out of frustration.

"Keep pressing. It isn't going to come any faster," she said sarcastically.

"Pipe down!" I snapped. I smiled when the lift doors opened, pushing her in to it.

"I can't believe you're doing this," she hissed at me.

I placed my arms either side of the lift doors. "You knew this would happen, even if it wasn't this weekend. It could have been five years down the line. It still would have always been her," I said before the lift doors closed.

She went to speak, but I held my hand up to silence her, turned my back, and walked away.

I looked past my room to see Freya sitting against the hotel wall, slumped on the floor. I jogged over to her and sat down next to her, my eyes searching her face. Her eye was bleeding and red.

"Geez, Freya. Your eye." I brushed my thumb across it, and she winced. "We should sort this out. Come," I demanded as I started to get up, but she grabbed my hand and pulled me back down next to her. "Please, just sit with me." A small, half smile appeared on her face.

"Baby, I'm so sorry. I left the room to speak to reception. Chloe told me she would be gone by the time I got back." I sighed.

Freya just nodded. "I text you as I hadn't heard from you. I thought you'd changed your mind," she mumbled. I watched as she unbent her crossed legs then kicked her Converse together, pouting.

"Never, Freya. I told you. I don't want to lose you again," I said quietly. She just sat there, saying nothing. I took the opportunity to speak. "Honestly, Freya. I don't. This past year has been hell." I sighed, her silence still deafening. "Yes, Chloe was more than a date, but I made it very obvious that it was just a 'thing'." I looked at her, searching for a response from her, but nope. She continued to stare at the wall ahead. "Chloe knew this was going to happen, especially knowing what would happen if I saw you. She was my

84

therapy in a way, after everything. I didn't want to tell my mum and Ava as I didn't want them to hate me. They love you so much." Her eyes flicked up at me. She went to speak, but I carried on. "But not as much as I do." My eyes widened. I stared so deeply into her eyes, searching for her soul, wishing it would come back to me. I moved closer to her, steadying my breath. "I really do," I whispered, my lips brushing against hers. "Come on. Let's continue with our day. But before the fun starts, let's sort your eye out."

She smiled, and I held out my hand to help her off the floor. Once she was up, we walked towards my room.

"She was a crazy bitch," Freya mumbled as we walked into my room. I walked in front of her, grabbing a wet cloth then slumping down onto my bed, eyeing her up and down. She looked cute in her white t-shirt, skinny jeans, and Converse.

She walked seductively over to me, swaying her hips. "What a morning eh?" she said as she stood in front of me, wrapping her arms around my neck and pushing herself in between my legs.

I reached up and pressed the cloth to her eye, keeping it there for a few moments. She kept her eyes on me, leaning down slightly and placing her full lips over mine, kissing me gently. She sent goosebumps over every inch of my skin as she played with the hair on the nape of my neck. I wrapped my hand around her waist as our kiss grew more passionate. Kissing her was the best feeling. I pulled away abruptly. I just wanted to talk to her. Make up for lost time.

"Can we just talk? As much as I want to take my rage out on you," I said, flirting with her. I did want to take my rage out on her, make her scream my name again and again.

"Talk?" she questioned me, confusion all over her face.

"Because, we've never done this. We've never spent the day together just talking. I don't want this relationship to be based solely on sex. We have a better connection than that. Don't get me wrong, the sex is out of this world." A big grin graced my face as I looked up at her. I pulled my bottom lip in between my teeth before lying back on the bed, propping myself up on my elbows then patting the bed next to me. "Come," I said, lust lacing my voice. She sat down next to me, huffing. "Oh, baby, don't sulk." I picked her hand up and kissed it. "I promise I will satisfy your every need later. We've got the whole day together," I said smoothly.

She replied to my words with a pout. "So, what do you want to talk about, Mr Cole?" she asked, emphasizing my name. She rolled on her side and rested her hand on the side of her face so she was leaning on her elbow.

I sighed at her, a small smile creeping onto my face. "I don't know off the top of my head. I just wanted to chill with you." I laughed. She raised her eyebrows at me. "Stop pressuring me!" I said loudly before letting out a roar of a laugh, and she laughed with me.

I loved listening to her laugh; it was one of the best sounds in the world. After a few moments, I started talking again. I just needed to get some things off my chest. "I really am sorry about before, baby," I said. She went to answer but I pressed my index finger up to her lips, silencing her. "You didn't deserve anything I put you through. I never meant for this all to get this far. Yes, my original plan was to get revenge because of how Aimee treated me, but from that first moment I saw you, I don't know why I didn't. I was a coward and I just want you to know how sorry I am. You do forgive me, don't you?"

I could tell she was uncomfortable with our conversation, but I needed to know she was okay with this.

"Carter," she said quietly, as if she was trying to process it all.

"Please forgive me." I crawled off the bed and knelt down on my knees, literally begging her.

"Carter, get up." She smirked at me.

"I won't until you tell me you forgive me," I teased.

"Yes! I forgive you. If I didn't, I wouldn't be here." She rolled her eyes. "Please get up."

I leant up and kissed her forehead. "And I promise you, the next time I'm on my knees will be when I am asking you to become my wife." I winked.

***

The afternoon was just what we needed, cuddling and talking about anything that popped into our heads. It wasn't all about what had happened, even though somehow it seemed to always go back to that, but I tried to change the course of the chat by giving her a little kiss here and there. But I just wanted to say one last thing before we could move on.

"As much as lying here doing nothing and chatting has been lovely, we actually do need to have a serious talk," I said quietly. She nodded in agreement then went to speak. I shook my head. "No, my darling. It's my turn to talk." She widened her eyes then threw me a smirk. I sat up, crossing my legs, sitting opposite her. I put my hands on her thighs, giving them a little squeeze, and she placed her hands over the top of mine. They looked tiny compared to mine.

"I need you back in my life. Not like this. Not like before," I choked. I didn't realise how hard this would actually be. "I can't lose you again." She rubbed her thumb across the back of my knuckles. "I kicked myself as soon as I left you in Elsworth, in that prick's arms," I said with rage clear in my tone. I took a deep breath, mentally counting in my head. "I love you more than you will ever know. I know this is one of the first times I'm telling you this, but I do. I fucking love you. I don't want to be with anyone else. I want to marry you, have babies with you, and do all the grown up stuff." I looked at her, searching her face for something.

"Wow. Okay, I wasn't expecting that," she said. "Can you just give me a few moments to process this? It's a lot to take in." She slid off the bed and walked around the room. I could see her mind ticking, her fingers up at her lips. She took some deep, slow breaths as she made her way to the hotel window, looking out at the city beneath her.

I rose slowly from the bed and walked behind her, wrapping my arms round her before turning her to face me. "Please, don't freak out. This has been eating me up since I left you. The amount of times I wanted to call and tell you, but you wouldn't answer. I knew you were going to be here. Laura told me. I told her not to tell you because I knew you wouldn't have come and I needed to see you. I love you. I know you feel the same. Please tell me you feel the same."

Her eyebrows furrowed, her mouth slightly open as she tried to take it all in. She closed her eyes for a few minutes, then took a big breath. "I love you too. I've loved you since our first date. You've broken my heart over and over again. I honestly don't think it could take anymore, Carter. You are my person. My person I want to spend my life with, but I need this to slow down. It's been a day. One whole day and we're back here again. Carter, this can't fuck up again. This needs to be for real. No more of these 'flavours of the months'. I told you once, I'm not that girl. If you want me and only me, and I want you and only you, then we will be fine. We're destined to be with each other. I feel like I've just been walking this Earth searching for you without realizing. My soul needs you, and so does my body." Her lips parted slightly as my breath caught. I noticed her little hint, about her body needing me.

I needed her. We needed to connect.

"I promise you, you and me, just us two. I have only felt

alive since meeting you. Freya, I love you." My eyes glazed over. I moved towards her, my mouth finding hers, my tongue exploring hers. I couldn't get enough. She moaned, which sent a signal straight to my cock, hardening it even more. I entwined my hands in her hair, tugging gently. I pulled her head back and started kissing her neck with soft, gentle kisses, nipping occasionally. Her hands ran down my t-shirt, then underneath, tracing out every inch of my torso. She pulled one hand out, slowly running her finger along the waistband of my jogging bottoms. A smirk crossed her face as she dropped to her knees.

Fuck if that wasn't a turn on in itself.

She tugged hungrily on my trousers, pulling them down then freeing me. She flicked her tongue across the head of my cock, teasing me. I let out a low groan then took a deep breath as she took all of me into her mouth. Her full lips looked fucking delicious around me, then she slowly pulled me out and ran her tongue up and down me from base to tip. She was completely undoing me. She flicked her tongue again on the tip of me.

"Stop," I said. "I don't want to come like this. Plus, we're in front of a window," I said, looking down at her with a wicked grin.

She stood up and put both hands on my chest, balancing herself, tiptoeing so her mouth was next to mine. "Don't be such a wimp," she whispered.

"A wimp? Oh, you wait."

CHAPTER ELEVEN

I stood still, my bottom half on show, and burned my eyes into hers. "Take your clothes off," I demanded. "Just leave your knickers on." I smirked.

"Take your clothes off" she replied, cockiness all over her face. And I did just that, peeling my t-shirt off so I was naked in front of her.

"Your turn, Miss Greene," I said as I walked closer to her. "Off. Now."

I watched as she slowly stripped for me, taking her t-shirt off and throwing it on the floor, her sun-kissed skin glowing in the light of the Paris sun. Her tits looked amazing in her white bra. I wanted to strip her, but I also wanted to savour every. Single. Minute of her doing it.

She undid her jeans, sliding them down her thick thighs before kicking them across the room. She slowly un-did her bra and stood with it, dangling it in her hand.

"You're looking good, Freya," I told her. I bit my lip as I watched her drop her bra to the floor. I was rock hard for her. "My, oh my. What a sight," I said in a low voice.

I didn't want to come across as desperate, but I needed her so bad.

I ran my fingertip from her shoulder, down past her breast, down her belly, then slowly down between her legs. I could feel how soaked she was already. I had only just touched her. I slowly caressed her through her lace thong, small, fuckable moans leaving her mouth.

I covered her mouth with my hand. "Shh. Don't make a sound," I whispered in her ear.

I spun her around, pushing her towards the floor to ceiling window so she was looking out over the city. I stood behind her, pressing myself into her as I did. I placed her hands either side of the window. She kept them there.

I ran my finger under her bum cheek creases, down to her thighs, then back up, pressing my hand against her thighs, gesturing for her to open her legs wider. She obeyed. I went back to trace the creases of her perfectly peached arse. I stopped then moved my hand underneath her, cupping her soaked sex in my hand then pushed my middle finger through the lace of her panties and slowly into her. She moaned as I started to caress her insides, curling my fingers slightly, hitting her delicate spot again and again. I felt her start to tighten around me, so I slowly pulled my finger out, then pulled her thong to the side, revealing that hot, toned arse. "Oh, I'm a lucky bastard," I muttered as I continued caressing her bum. I moved down to my knees as I started to plant gentle kisses on both of her cheeks, nipping her occasionally. When I did nip, she threw her head back, her hair falling down her back. I ran my hands up her thighs slowly, pushing them further apart then grabbed her hips, pulling them back towards me so her front was forward and her back was arched. I moved in between her legs and pressed my tongue into her core, flicking my tongue over her clit. I slowly continued tasting every inch of her. I couldn't get enough. I pushed my tongue into her deeper as she moaned in appreciation. I tightened my grip on her hip, and with my free hand, I slipped two fingers into her soaked opening, pushing deep inside her and feeling her clamp around me. I continued the slow tongue strokes on the most sensitive part of her body as my fingers plunged into her faster. I stopped then started kissing her cheeks again, her moans getting louder, my fingers getting deeper.

"Stop," she moaned, barely able to speak. I ignored her, enjoying this way too much to stop, my mouth back over her. "Carter, please!"

Again, I ignored her. She was getting close. Her legs started to tremble. I slowed down my fingers, but still pushed them deeper into her then I stopped abruptly. I stood up from my knees, leaning over her back so my mouth was next to her ears. "I'm going to fuck you now."

I smiled as I heard the pants leaving her mouth; she was so turned on. I looked in between her legs to see the glisten. I steadied myself behind her, holding onto her hip and using my other hand to position the head of my cock at her opening. I teased for a moment, slowly entering the tip, stretching her before I thrust into her slowly. I then placed my other hand on her hip, picking up the pace and thrusting into her hard. Her hips moved with me, which made a growl escape my lips. I began to move faster into her, the sound of my skin and hers together as I thrust into her deep, hitting her spot again and again. Fuck, she was so tight. She felt like pure ecstasy. Her fingers clawed the wall as she was getting close. Her tightening and clamping around me only pushed my orgasm closer. I let go of one of her hips and grabbed her ponytail, pulling her head back as far as I could as I continued to hit into her deeper.

Her legs were trembling as she cried out, "I'm going to come!"

She moaned as I groaned, coming with her, feeling myself empty inside her. I stilled for a moment, a shudder leaving me. She was still facing the wall, panting. Her skin glistened from the sweat, her arousal apparent on her, and my arousal slowly making its way down her leg. I instantly went hard at the sight. She was a fucking delight.

We lay in bed, both still naked, completely entwined in each other with her lying under my arm. "I'm hungry. Can we get room service?" she asked.

"Why don't we go into the hotel restaurant and eat? It's your last night."

"I don't want to get dressed, and to be honest, I don't want to run into Morgan and Courtney." She shuffled and nuzzled into me more. She smelt divine, like sex, me, and Chanel no. 5. "Plus, this is sooo much better than sitting in a restaurant."

I tutted at her comment. "Fine. Let's order room service, but as soon as we're home, I'm taking you out," I said, picking the phone up.

When I'd ordered, I put the phone down, and Freya let out a sigh. She sat up in bed, shuffling towards the headboard, and I moved up with her.

"What's wrong?" I asked.

"I'm worried."

"Why are you worried?" I furrowed my brow. "What if this is just the honeymoon period? We couldn't make it work before, so what's to say it will work this time?"

"Freya." I shuffled closer to her, scooping her up into my embrace. "I told you, I won't lose you again. This is it. You're stuck with me. I will make you my wife," I said sternly. I leant into her neck, kissing her. "I promised you, Freya. It's just me and you."

She wriggled out of my arms then slipped out of bed and into the bathroom. I heard the door lock.

Confused, I moved to the edge of the bed. I gave her a few minutes before walking over to the bathroom, knocking gently on the door. "Everything okay, baby?" I asked, concerned.

"Yeah, fine. Just needed the loo."

"No problem," I said as I walked away from the bathroom, giving her some privacy.

I put my jogging bottoms back on and climbed onto the bed, waiting for room service. I was starving. I wondered whether I had scared her off, or if she just needed a moment because it all of a sudden got a bit too heavy. Was she actually going to come back out again? I sighed, tapping my thumb on my thigh as I waited for her.

I heard her footsteps. Shooting up quickly, I stood by the door, waiting for her. I let out a relieved breath as I heard the door unlock. "You sure you're okay?" I asked as she walked out. She was wrapped in a hotel robe. She could have been dressed in a black bag and still looked beautiful.

"I'm fine. It's just... this afternoon has been a bit of a whirlwind." She smiled at me, her eyes glistening. "I've gone from coming here, worried I was going to see you, to then seeing you. We slept together, and you poured your heart out to me. It's not even been twenty-four hours. I just feel overwhelmed. My brain can't register what's happening." I could see the sheer panic in her eyes; they were searching mine for reassurance.

"Baby, I'm sorry. I didn't mean for you to feel like that. I just needed to tell you everything." I rested my forehead against hers. "You've changed me. I've never felt like this before and I'm absolutely terrified I will lose you again." My eyes looked deep into hers.

I felt vulnerable. I couldn't work out the feelings that were coming out. She wrapped her arms around my waist and snuggled into my chest. Just the feel of her on me calmed me down, my heart instantly slowing, my shoulders relaxing.

"Let's just take one day at a time, yeah?" Freya suggested. We stood for a moment in silence when there was a knock on the suite door.

"That must be dinner," I said smoothly, pulling Freya's arms from my waist then walking towards the door and taking the dinner plates from him. I closed the suite door with my foot. "Hungry?" I asked.

"Famished," she said, sitting back on the bed and waiting for her food. Her eyes lit up when she lifted the silver lid, revealing steak, chips, and peppercorn sauce. I wonder if she realised I had ordered this because I cooked this dinner for her on our first date at my house. I looked over as she pushed the plate away, clearly full. She got up and walked over to the desk, grabbing a bottle of the hotel water and taking a few sips.

"You okay, babe?" I asked.

"Fine, just ate too fast." She rolled her eyes.

"Glad you enjoyed it." I smiled.

"I should really go. Need to catch up with Courtney. No doubt I have loads of work to do," she muttered as she placed the bottle of water down on the side.

"Don't go. Stay the night. You leave tomorrow," I said, pulling a sad face and giving my best puppy dog eyes then winking.

"Oh, I don't know. I should really get back." She pulled her phone out of her back pocket, giving it a glance. I walked towards her, her eyes devouring me.

"You really shouldn't," I said seductively, grinning. She couldn't argue; I didn't let her. I kissed her, pushing her back on the desk, lifting her onto it then pushing her back again slightly. I ran my hand down to her legs, pushing them apart then moving in between them. I placed my hands round her face, cradling it. My heart was beating against my ribcage as our kiss became deeper. I couldn't wait to bury myself inside her again; I always felt hard around her. My cock bulged against my trousers. I felt so full, even though I couldn't be. It was just her. I could see she needed me; she needed me like I needed her. I kissed her neck, planting them down to her collarbone. I undid the tie on her robe; I needed to touch her. I pushed the dressing gown off then kissed her bare shoulder. Freya tried to pull the dressing gown away, but I wouldn't let her. She looked completely undone. She still had her just-fucked look. She was fucking stunning. I smoothed my hands over her skin, as if I was following a treasure map. I moved them slowly down her hips, then to her thighs. I found where I wanted to be. I pushed my fingers into her, teasing her on every slow, deep thrust. She was so ready for me, always. She bit her lip as she watched me pushing into her. I ran my spare hand up, my fingers tracing along her jawline then tilting her chin back. I covered her mouth with mine. My kiss was fierce, hungry. I was lost in the moment. My fingers were still inside her, making her come undone under my touch and I didn't want to be anywhere else but there. I pulled away from her, the moans intoxicating me, hypnotising me into some sort of frenzy. I flicked my tongue harshly over her hard nipples, sucking and licking while my fingers thrust fast into her. Her moans grew louder, my kisses smothering every exposed part of her body. I was completely lost in her. She was mine; I loved her.

CHAPTER TWELVE

I was awoken when I heard the clatter of cups and teapots. I slowly opened my eyes to see her standing in nothing by my t-shirt from last night, making us a cup of tea. She looked over her shoulder, smirking at me. She was glowing, her auburn hair pulled into a messy ponytail, her grey eyes glistening at me.

I stretched, still tucked under the duvet.

"Good morning, handsome," she purred, walking over to me with a cup of tea. She leaned down, planting a soft peck on my lips. I breathed in her scent; a mix of sex, and her Chanel no. 5. It was intoxicating.

I sat up, taking the tea from her. "Good morning, beautiful." My mouth broke into a smile as I took a sip of the hot tea. "Mmm, that is a good cup of tea. I could get used to this." I winked at her.

She picked her own cup up from the desk then sat next to me in the bed, crossing her leg underneath her. I leant up, kissing her forehead.

"So, what's going to happen when we're back home?" she asked me. "I leave in a few hours, then it's back to life."

I reached over, putting my cup on the bedside table before facing her. "I think we should live together," I said.

I could see the doubt on her face. "Do you not think it's a bit soon?' she questioned me. "I only said last night that I want to take things one step at a time and you're saying about us living together. I just meant with us. What are we going to do?"

I could hear the panic in her voice. I reached out and took her hand. "Please calm down." I shook my head, smiling at her. "I'm not saying we should move in together right away, but I do want to live with you."

She bit her lip, silent. A few moments later, she said, "One step at a time." She put her hand over mine. "I need to pack," she said then slowly pulled her hand from mine.

I let out a sigh. "Fine. I suppose I have to let you go." I reached over to pick up my tea again. She put hers down on the bedside unit next to her and threw the duvet back. Just as she swung her legs round to get off the bed, I wrapped my arms around her and pulled her back into me. "But first, I want to ask you something." Her lips parted, her breathing becoming faster, her eyes boring into mine. She didn't break contact, not even to blink. "Freya, please be my girlfriend? My one and only?" A big smile spread across my face. I was nervous, shaking inside and hoping she couldn't sense it.

She didn't keep me waiting long.

"Of course!" she said in an elated scream, pulling her into my embrace.

"Did you not want to think about your answer?" I teased.

She shook her head, a smirk on her face. She placed both her hands either side of her face, moving closer to me. She stopped just as our lips were about to touch. Her breathing calmed as she watched me. She looked at my chest, watching my heart thumping through my skin. She kept her hands on the sides of my face, moving closer to into me, this time kissing me. I felt the electric course through me at her touch. I was instantly hard from her. She pulled away then took my lip between her teeth, making me let out a low groan.

"Tut tut, Miss Greene." I smirked. I put my right hand round the back of her and head and pulled her back in. She dropped her hands from my face then grabbed the thin bed sheet that separated our bodies. A sweet grin appeared on her face, and she kneeled up, tugging the sheet away hungrily. Her eyes widened as she drank in every inch of me. She sat back down slowly and started thrusting back and forward ever so slowly. She was teasing me, the minx. She shuffled and lifted herself ever so slightly as she repositioned herself over me, this time taking all of me. Her eyes closed slowly as she enjoyed the pleasure rippling through her. She moaned as I thrust into her deeply, her hips moving faster on me. I pushed her t-shirt up in my sex haze so I could grip onto her hips. I opened my legs slightly so I could hit into her deeper, moving with her easier. Every time she moved her hips forward, I matched her movement as she moaned out louder. Her lips came down to meet mine, crashing into me hungrily. Her eyes opened while she watched me crumble underneath her. My breath hitched as I felt my impending orgasm about to hit. She slowed slightly and started circling her hips. I inhaled a sharp, deep breath through my teeth as she continued. I reached up to kiss her, but she pulled back slightly, shaking her head. She kept her eyes on mine, watching me. I tightened my grip on her hips as I forcefully thrust into her, hitting her sensitive spot again and again. She started with the control, and just like that, I took the control back. I knew she was close, but I wasn't letting her come yet. I lifted her off me and flipped her, putting her on all fours. I pushed her back down so her arse and hips were high in the air. Fuck, what a sight. Her soaked core glistened with her arousal. It was such a turn on. I parted her legs a bit more so I could push into her even deeper. I wanted to feel every part of her. I didn't give her any warning, no teasing. I thrust into her fast and hard hitting her deeply and harshly. She tightened around me, clamping onto me. My name left her sweet fucking mouth as she cried out, and that delicious moan pushed me over the edge, releasing an intense orgasm that crashed through me. I let up my grip on her hips, her legs trembling beneath me. I stilled for a moment before leaning over her and whispering, "What a wonderful way to start the morning," before spanking her peachy arse cheek.

After lying in our post-sex state, Freya left the bed for the shower. I didn't want her to go home without me. I wanted to stay with her and never leave her again. I couldn't be without her anymore. Ever.

I heard the bathroom door open. I was lying on my stomach, dealing with some work emails, still naked with the bed sheet over me. It had fallen slightly so my arse was on show. I took my eyes off my phone before looking over at her, flashing her my best smile followed by a wink. She had a towel wrapped around her, and a smaller one wrapped on her head. How was it possible for her to always look so beautiful?

"Not now, Mr Cole. You've had enough. I need to pack. I have a job and life to go back to – I'm not rich like you." She scowled at me.

I rolled over, pulling the sheet with me, not wanting to give her an eyeful. "Oh, you will be one day. You will be rich beyond your means."

She just stared at me. She ignored my remark before turning her back on me. She pulled the towel from her head and rough dried her hair before slipping on her jeans from last night, then her t-shirt over her head. She walked over to me in the bed, leaning down and kissing me. Just as our lips touched, I pulled her on top of me.

"No!" she screamed, laughing. "Let me go. I need to go!" She wriggled to get out of my vice-like grip. I laughed at her, a deep belly chuckle. She stopped struggling for a moment and watched me, her eyes consumed with me.

"What are you staring at?" I stopped laughing to ask her.

She didn't say anything, just pulled herself away, sitting on the edge of the bed before responding, "You. I love watching you happy and laughing." She leaned down and kissed me again. "Bye. I will see you when you're home." She got up off the bed. "Whenever that will be." She rolled her eyes after making her comment.

I muttered, "Please don't go," but she was already at the door, closing it and not looking back.

I threw myself back on the bed, I instantly felt agitated that she had gone. I pulled myself off the bed and walked towards the bathroom; I needed a shower. After my long shower, I took my chances of seeing if she was still in her room. I didn't even know what time her flight was. Mine was that evening, which was annoying. I texted James to see if he could get me out of there any sooner. I didn't want to be there any longer than I needed to be. I didn't want to be away from Freya any longer than I had to be.

I pulled my clothes on, grabbing my phone and key card

and left the room, walking towards Freya's. I knocked on the door, praying she was still there. I smiled when I heard it unlocking. Courtney stood there, a stupid grin on her face. I looked past her and saw my beautiful Freya.

"Morning, Courtney." I smiled at her, my heart racing when I saw Freya walking towards me, pecking me on the cheek.

"What are you doing here? We're leaving in ten." She looked at the time on her phone before shoving it in her back pocket.

"I wanted to come and say goodbye. I'm on a later flight. My plane is here, but due to the amount of flights going out today, we can't get a slot until later on." I sighed. "Which means it will be a few hours before I get to see you again." I wrapped my arms around her and pulled her into me, nuzzling into her neck. I quickly let go of her when I saw Morgan approaching.

"Morgan." I greeted him in a deep, blunt grunt.

"Carter." He carried the same tone.

Freya looked over her shoulder at Courtney, Courtney throwing her an awkward half-smile.

"I just overheard you saying your plane can't get a slot until later on, is that right?" Morgan asked.

"Yes, unfortunately." I sighed, letting down the guard I had up.

"Well, I have space on my plane if you want to jump on." He smiled at me, and I saw Freya and Courtney instantly relax.

"Only if you're sure. It would make my life a little easier." I let out a small chuckle.

"Of course. Not a problem," he muttered before stepping towards me and shaking my hand.

I watched as he proceeded to walk towards Courtney. "We're leaving in five." He leaned down and kissed her forehead. "See you in a mo." He winked at Courtney before walking towards the door. "Nice to see you smiling again, Freya," he said to her politely before walking into the hallway.

I was slightly pissed off that he said that, but I could understand why he said it. It made my heart hurt knowing I had caused her sadness and misery. I was secretly grateful she had Morgan and Courtney on her side.

Morgan and I were standing at the hotel reception, waiting to check us out. The guy was dealing with another couple.

"Thanks for this again, Morgan. You've saved me a lot of bother," I admitted.

"Not a problem. We're all heading the same way," he said, tapping his room card on the reception desk.

"And thank you for you and Courtney being there for Freya." I felt vulnerable talking to Morgan. I didn't get intimidated easily, but Morgan was one of those people who did intimidate me. His ice blue stared, burning through me.

"Anything for Freya. Yes, she is my employee but Courtney and I care for her a lot." He nodded at me

"I know."

"Just because we've spoken civilly for the first time in months, don't think you aren't still my rival." He let out a deep   laugh.

"Ha. Wouldn't want it any other way." I laughed with him, kicking my trainer against the base of the desk. Thank fuck the receptionist arrived.

"Afternoon, gentlemen. How can I be of assistance to you?" he asked, smiling.

Once we were checked out, we walked over to the girls, who were staring at us as if we were an endangered species. They both knew we were rivals so this must've been weird for them.

"Our car is outside," Morgan said to Courtney before taking her hand and walking slowly outside. We followed.

"I can't wait to get home and back to normality." She smiled up at me, lacing her fingers in mine and squeezing my hand as she did.

After a long car journey, and us nearly missing our flight, we were finally on the plane. I saw Freya looking over at Morgan and Courtney who were snuggled up into each other. It must have been weird for him coming out of his marriage to Evangeline and now being with Courtney. But then again, it's nice for him to be free and able to be with who he wants. I placed my hand between Freya's thighs, my right hand resting on my knee. I smiled when Freya linked her arm through mine.

"Let's go home" I said as the plane took off.

After a short flight, we were back on home turf, and I must admit, it was good to be home.

We walked straight off the plane. Freya said goodbye to Courtney, pulling her in for a hug. I shook Morgan's hand and thanked him once again. We slipped straight into my waiting car with James. Freya's face lit up when she saw him. They exchanged pleasantries before he closed the door for us both.

"I'm looking forward to some alone time with you. Come back to the penthouse with me?" I asked. "Please."

She shook her head. "I can't." Her eyes darted to the floor, "I have to get ready for work tomorrow. I have washing to do, and I need to get Tilly from Erin."

I placed my finger up to her lips. "Shh. I will come back to yours then. I don't want to spend a moment away from you." I smiled.

"It's a mess at my place. No food is in, either. You know what I'm like." She giggled and nudged into me.

"We will stop at the shops and pick some food up. I'll cook."

"Oh, Carter. You don't have to do that."

"I want to. Then we can make the most of our evening." I winked at her.

"Can't wait," she said before biting her bottom lip. I squeezed her knee while we enjoyed the drive home.

I looked over at her when I heard her phone beep. It was Laura. Freya just rolled her eyes and closed the message. "You not going to reply?" I smirked at her.

"No. not yet. Let her stew. She knows what she she's done. I'm glad she intervened, obviously," she said. This time, it was her winking at me that sent a signal straight to my cock, waking him. "But she has pissed me off."

She looked back at her phone, bringing it up to her ear as she listened to a voicemail and smiled sweetly. It made me believe it must be her mum or dad. I was so nervous to see them again after what I did and how things were left.

"I'm going down to see my mum and dad soon. Wanna come?" she asked.

"Hmm, are you sure? Look what happened last time."

"Well, Mr Cole, that wouldn't have happened if you'd told me the truth from the start now, would it?" she replied bitterly. Couldn't blame her. It was my fault entirely.

I checked my phone to find an email from the company I was due to complete on which stirred my insides, pissing me off. I started tapping a response, letting out a deep sigh.

"What's wrong?" she asked, squeezing my knee gently.

"Nothing, babe. Just these arseholes in New York now deciding to change the deal." I shook my head. "Does my head in. All of that for them to now start negotiating just as the paperwork is due to be signed."

She leaned across the seat, pecking me on the cheek. "Try and forget about it. I don't want it to ruin our night." She smiled at me.

That one small bit of affection instantly relaxed me, making me feel so much better. I didn't know how she did it, but she made my soul alight. She had brought me back to life, back from my darkness that I never thought I would get out of. I thought I was going to fall so far down into a black hole that I would never be found again. Just when I was about to give up, I found her. She reconnected with my empty soul. My soul was searching for her, but it needed to be her to find mine. I needed her forgiveness, and I finally had it.

CHAPTER THIRTEEN

We pulled up outside the little shops by Freya's apartment and quickly nipped inside. I wanted to cook something quick and tasty; I didn't really want to spend all night cooking in her kitchen. I would much rather spend my evening with my head between her legs, enjoying her sweet taste and making her come over and over again. I smirked as I pictured her coming undone from my tongue. Such a perfect sight. I snapped out of it when she spoke.

"Anything you fancy in particular?" she asked.

"You," I said bluntly.

She blushed, her gorgeous tanned skin turning a shade of red. "No, seriously. What do you fancy?"

"What about pasta? Prawn, lemon, chilli with linguine?" I suggested. She licked her lips in agreement. "It's nice and light so we won't be bloated." I winked at her.

I walked towards the wine chiller, grabbing us a bottle of Sauvignon. It seemed to be the only decent wine in there.

I threw my cash at the cashier and quickly ushered Freya into the back of James' car.

We pulled up outside Freya's shitty apartment. I couldn't wait to get her out of there and living with me. Okay, the area wasn't bad, but I didn't like the fact that she was this far from me. It would have been worse if me and Ethan hadn't become friendly, as such, so I knew she had him looking out for her. I should message him, fill him in on what happened since we last spoke a few months ago.

Freya politely said goodnight to James as she waited for me kerbside.

"Thank you, James. I will call you in the morning. Enjoy your night off." I shook his hand then gently patted him on the back. I liked to give him the night off when I could so he and Julia could enjoy some alone time together.

We trailed up the stairs together before Freya pushed past me to unlock her door. She smiled as she took her little flat in. She seemed glad to be home. I followed her and placed the bags on the worktop. She was right, it was a mess, but I didn't care. All I cared about was that I was with her, alone, finally.

She disappeared into her bedroom with her small suitcase. I followed like a lost puppy. I stood close behind her, breathing her in as if she was my drug. I couldn't get enough of her. I wrapped my arms around her small waist, my hands running round to her stomach then planting soft, gentle kisses on her neck. She tipped her head back, her face tilted slightly as she enjoyed the feeling of my lips on her skin. I could feel her smile.

"Hey, steady on. You promised me dinner and I am starved." She giggled as she pulled my hands away and turned to face me.

"Of course, my lady," I teased and walked into the kitchen, following her orders as I left her to unpack.

I started unpacking the shopping, placing the bits I needed on the side in the order I needed them in. Hey, I was no Gordon Ramsay, but I knew how to cook pasta and prawns. I grabbed the chilled white wine and poured her a big glass, placing it on the small breakfast bar amongst her letters and magazines so it was ready for her. For some reason, a thought sprang into my head. I couldn't help but wonder if she had been with anyone since me. Not that I could talk, I had been with Chloe. I hated every minute of it, but she filled a void that needed filling until I had my babe back in my arms. I felt bitter as the thoughts consumed me, thinking of another man touching what was mine. Making her feel things that only I should be able to make her feel. I quickly dismissed the thoughts that were slowly souring my mood and poisoning my heart as she walked towards me.

I handed her the glass of wine, watching her take a big mouthful and letting out a moan of appreciation as it slid down her throat. She perched on one of the stools under her breakfast bar and watched me start to cook.

"How hot do you like it?" I asked as I started finely slicing the chilli, facing her and throwing her a little smirk. My dirty thoughts were getting the better of me.

"Oh, I like it very hot, Mr Cole," she chirped back.

"We will see how hot you like it after dinner. Now, back to my question. How hot do you want your pasta?"

"Just a few chillis, please. Don't want my tongue to catch alight."

"Dinner will be done in five. Pour me a glass of wine, please, and make some room at the breakfast bar for me."

She hopped off the breakfast bar and quickly scooped up the letters and mags and placed them on the arm of the sofa in the living room. I threw the prawns in to cook in the chilli and lemon sauce that was simmering. Freya walked to the fridge, grabbing the chilled wine and pouring me a glass. She sniffed in appreciation and licked her lips again at the sight of the food. Once the prawns were cooked, I tossed the linguine in the sauce then added the prawns. I served two big helpings into mis-matched bowels and served them on the breakfast bar. I squeezed a little bit of lemon over the top and handed her a knife and fork before taking my seat next to her.

"Enjoy." I beamed at her.

I took a mouthful of wine. It wasn't bad for a cheap one from the corner shop. I took a mouthful of food and groaned as the taste hit my taste buds. I couldn't help but boast, "Oh. I am good. I am so good."

"All right. Pipe down, Gordon Ramsay." She chuckled, which made me laugh too, helping lift my mood.

Once dinner was finished, I needed a shower. I went to tidy but Freya shooed me away and told me she would do it. I was in my own little world, rinsing my hair when I saw the shower curtain pull back. Fuck me, the sight of her completely naked standing there. Her long auburn hair tumbled down her sides. She stepped in, wrapping her little arms around me tightly and planting soft, wet kisses along my shoulders. She reached up on her tiptoes to continue her trail of kisses up my neck. I relaxed, pushing all the negativity from earlier well away. Her kisses continued over my wet skin, making me rock solid for her. I spun around, cradling her beautiful fucking face, pulling her under the cascading water with me. She placed her tiny hands onto my toned forearms, gripping me tightly. I kissed her softly on her plump lips, my hands still around her face. My tongue pushed into her mouth slowly, teasing hers. I felt her silver grey eyes on me which made me open mine. I was completely lost in the moment, as was she. She closed her eyes as I pushed my lips onto hers, this time our kiss hungrier. My tongue was forceful in her mouth. She matched the same teasing rhythm. She let go of my forearms and ran them down my body, stopping just before she got to my groin area. I slowly ran my fingers down to my cock before placing it

116

into her tiny hand. She smiled as she saw the beads of arousal on the tip. She moved her hand up and down my shaft, pumping me slowly. I wanted her, so fucking bad. I quickly looked to see where I could take her; we only had the wall to the side of me due to her only having an over bath shower. Her hand started pumping faster. I craned my neck down, taking her bottom lip between my teeth and biting down hard which caused a whimper from her. She tightened her grip around me, picking up her speed. I let out a deep moan, throwing my head back. I snapped my head forward, grabbing her jaw with my free hand and kissing her hard. I wanted her to feel me on her lips for the coming days. I reluctantly let go of her jaw and tightened my hand round her wrist, signalling for her to stop. I wanted her now. All of her. I stepped out of the shower-bath, taking her hand. She followed in a lust-filled state.

We stood on the bath mat, staring at each other. I traced my finger up the inside of her thigh, then pushing her thigh up, I placed it on the edge of the bath, her other still on the floor. I smiled down at her. She was panting already and I had hardly touched her.

I dropped to my knees and pushed my tongue between her folds with no warning, in a slow and teasing manner. She gripped onto the basin, steadying herself, while her other hand found my hair, fisting it tightly which only spurred me on to push my tongue deeper into her, flicking my tongue across her sensitive clit. Her eyes flitted down, watching my tongue spear in and out of her at a slow pace. She was such a fucking turn on. Even more so now that she was watching me. I slipped a finger into her soaked core, plunging it in deeper, but keeping up the slow and tantalizing rhythm when she tightened around me, before reaching her sweet release.

I led her to the bedroom. She went to grab a towel when I picked her up, stopping her from covering her glorious fucking body. She wrapped her legs tightly around me as I pushed her into the wall. I dropped one hand and positioned myself at her opening before thrusting into her hard. She gasped as I slowed down. She dug her nails into my back in agreement as I continued to sink into her slowly and deeply.

I was getting close, as was she. I picked up the pace as I hit into her faster and deeper. I squeezed her bum and buried my head into her neck as I thrust into her so fast I thought I was going to have a heart attack. She clamped around me, coming hard and moaning out my name loudly as I came inside her, my cock twitching. I took a moment to calm my breathing before walking her to the bed and dropping her from my waist then collapsing next to her in our post orgasm bliss.

"Satisfied, Miss Greene?" I grinned.

"Always, Mr Cole." She grinned back. Fuck, when she says my full name.

"I'm exhausted. I need a good night's sleep," I said. "I

couldn't sleep when we were apart. Now you're back, I feel much more relaxed."

"Me too." She rolled over onto me, kissing me on the forehead. "I'm just going to lock up," she said as she crawled off the bed and picked my dirty t-shirt up before pulling it over her head. She bought it up to her nose sneakily and sniffed, smiling as she did, then walked down the hallway. I moved slightly so I was lying in bed and decided to close my eyes for a minute, just to rest them. The next thing I knew, I was plunged into a deep sleep. This was where I needed to be. Back with her. Forever and always.

I woke slightly disorientated as I rubbed my eyes. I smiled as soon as I saw my beautiful Freya next to me. I placed soft kisses over her cheeks, moving onto her nose then down to her lips. Her eyelashes fluttered on her skin before her grey eyes were on mine. "I've got to go, baby. Big meeting with these idiots from New York."

I didn't want to go to work. I wanted to crawl back into bed and spend the day with her.

She stretched, her naked body appearing from under her duvet. I was hard. I was always hard around her. "Oh, back to reality," she mumbled.

"I know. It sucks." I smiled. "But I promise, in a few weeks, we will have a weekend break. Just me and you," I said as I stood from the bed.

"That would be perfect." She smiled at me. "Have a

good day."

"You too. I'll call you later. We really need to sort out our living arrangements. Think about it, please." I winked at her. "Bye, baby," I said before walking out the door, hearing her shout "Bye" as I got to her flat door. A massive smile spread across my face.

James was waiting for me.

"Morning, James," I chirped as I sat back in the car.

"Morning, boss."

"I hope you had a nice evening off. I need to go back to the penthouse and get a suit on, then to the offices for nine for my meeting," I ordered.

"Not a problem, and yes, my evening was great, thank you," he replied.

Within half an hour, I was outside the penthouse. I instantly felt homesick without her. I told James to keep the car running; I would only be ten minutes. I ran straight up to my bedroom and into my wardrobe, grabbing my grey suit off the rail and stripping. I done my buttons up on my crisp white shirt before shrugging my suit jacket on, doing the two buttons up. I sprayed my aftershave and styled my hair and left the room, grabbing a banana from the kitchen before I headed out to the front door. I jumped straight into the car. James pulled off before I had even shut the door. I looked at the time. Eight thirty. Fuck.

I made my meeting by the skin of my teeth, sitting down with the douche from New York. This better not be a waste of my fucking time. By the time the meeting was over, I had managed to get him to agree to the terms after some gruelling back and forth negotiating. Plus, he wanted more money for his business which I signed through gritted teeth. I walked into my office and picked up my mobile, calling the local florist.

I ordered Freya a dozen red roses with a note saying; 'they say you only fall in love once, but that can't be true... every time I look at you, I fall in love all over again.' I needed her to know just how deep my feelings ran for her. I then text her telling her I would be outside her office at five. I silenced my phone and caught up with the carnage that was left for me while in Paris. Four thirty soon arrived. I had a phone call come in to my office phone, but I ignored it. I had a date with my queen and I wasn't going to be late. I walked out of our lavish offices to see James waiting for me. He always looked so smart, yet so relaxed. I was at her office at five p.m. on the dot. I waited a few minutes, but she still wasn't outside. I decided to call her.

"Hey, you," she purred.

"Hey, beautiful. I'm downstairs. You ready?" I asked.

"I wish. I have about half an hour left of work. Are you okay to wait? Please?"

ASHLEE ROSE

I let out a sigh followed by a chuckle. "I'll wait. Don't be long, or I'll come in there and take you," I said sternly. I wanted her to know I was serious.

"Okay, okay. Love you."

I heard the small gasp that came out of her mouth. That was the first time she had told me she loved me. My black heart exploded in my chest, the red starting to show once more.

"I love you too," I replied, a smile plastered over my face. I cut the phone off and sat watching my watch. Half hour had passed and she still wasn't outside.

"James, wait here," I snapped.

I walked into the office and past security, ignoring them completely when they questioned who I was. I hit the button on the lift and shot up to Freya's office. I walked into the lobby and around the corner, my eyes searching for her. Then I saw her. Her eyes widened as she saw me walking towards her. She checked her phone and then slowly stood.

"Oh my God. I am so sorry. I'm on the last section!"

"I'm hungry," I moaned.

"So am I. I promise I'm nearly done. I really don't want to piss Morgan off."

"Why would you piss him off?"

"Because he wants this contract done by tomorrow. Sorry, I've been told not to discuss with you." She grinned at me, knowing she was going to get my back up.

I ran my hand through my tousled hair, frustrated. "Did

he now?" I said, my eyes thin as I walked towards her, my eyes burning into hers.

"What is going through your head, Mr Cole?" she teased. She looked so fuckable. Her cleavage on show slightly in her tight white shirt, and that leather pencil skirt that I loved so fucking much.

"Oh, you don't want to know." I smiled and leaned down, kissing her. "As much as I want to take my frustration out on you here, especially on Morgan's desk..." I raised my eyebrows "I just want to get you home. I want to eat dinner with you and then take my time on you. Now, hurry up. This man needs food." I stepped away and put my hands in my pockets, looking around Morgan's office. I was not impressed. "You're wasted here" I said. "Come back and work for me." I smiled.

She laughed. "No way. Not yet, anyway. One step at a time." She winked at me. "Now, please, be quiet. I'm nearly finished."

I rolled my eyes. If she wasn't done in five, I was throwing her over my shoulder and taking her out of there.

CHAPTER FOURTEEN

We were finally in the car after she had made me wait another half an hour on top. I was now starving and hangry. She sighed with relief as James pulled away.

"I'm so glad to be out of the office. Morgan is so different to work with. I feel sorry for Courtney, having to deal with him in that mood."

"All the more reason for you to leave." I smiled.

"Carter," she said in a warning tone. I rolled my eyes at her. "What's for dinner?"

"Julia is preparing a roast. I was craving one. She cooks the best roast potatoes," I said fondly.

"I can't wait to try them. Love a roastie." She giggled.

I smiled when we pulled up outside the penthouse. I had just realised she hadn't been back here since we broke up. As we walked into the hallway of my home, the smell of roast beef hit my nostrils, making my stomach growl. I dismissed James for the evening, wishing him a good night.

We walked into the dining room.

"Evening, Mr Cole, Miss Greene. Dinner will be ready in ten," Julia said politely before attending to the dinner again.

"Thank you, Julia" I said warmly.

We sat down at the dining room table as Julia served our dinner.

"My mum and Ava are coming down in a few weeks. I would love for you to spend the weekend here. Maybe invite your mum and dad down. It would be nice for them to finally meet," I said, smiling.

"That would be lovely. I'll check with my parents." She returned my smile.

Freya thanked Julia as she finished serving. We lost ourselves in light chatter while we enjoyed every mouthful.

Once dinner was finished and we cleaned up, we made our way to the lounge. I pulled the French doors to then lit the fire before pouring myself and Freya a glass of red wine each. I had got changed. It felt good to be in my casual jogging bottoms and my t-shirt. Freya was wearing a tracksuit I had bought her before we split up. She lay with her head on my chest, my arms wrapped around her as I used the sofa arm to support me. She surprised me with what she said next, sitting up.

"I've been thinking about what you said, about moving

in." She tapped her nails on the side of her wine glass.

My heart was thumping. "Really?"

"Yes, really."

I leaned across the sofa and kissed her passionately, only pulling myself away due to excitement. "This is great! Will you move in here?" I asked.

"At the moment, yes, but honestly, Carter, I would like us to buy somewhere." She stopped, looking up at me. "Somewhere new."

"Of course. I completely understand. Let's take our time and find our perfect home." I scooted closer to her, stealing another kiss.

"Look, there is something I want to talk to you about," she said quietly, scooting away slightly, clearly nervous.

I looked her, my eyebrows pulled together as I kept my eyes on hers.

"Don't be worried. It's not bad," she assured me. "Go pour us another glass of wine, then we can talk."

I smiled nervously and walked into the kitchen, grabbing the bottle of wine and returning.

I sat back next to her, placing the bottle of red on the coffee table. I rubbed my hands together. My eyes felt wide, and my heart was beating rapidly in my chest I thought it was going to burst. She placed her hand on my knee and gave it a gentle squeeze. "Look, I just wanted to say sorry for the way I acted when everything came out. You know, back in Elsworth." She cleared her throat. I opened my mouth, ready to tell her she didn't need to say sorry. She wasn't the one who needed to apologise but she pressed her finger to my lips. "No, shh." She shook her head. "My turn to talk." She smiled weakly. "If we're going to move forward in this relationship, I need to get this off my chest."

I sat silent, waiting. My eyes darted to her knotted fingers.

"I should have followed you. I should have ignored everything and everyone and got in the car." She dropped her eyes, sighing. "Watching you drive away was like no other pain I had ever felt. My heart broke. I was trying to be strong, to prove a point to myself. I really don't know why. I should have just picked up the phone and called you, except I deleted and blocked your number. I shouldn't have let you go. The moment I did, I broke my own heart. I just didn't know how much I loved you, how much I needed you." My heart thumped. My beautiful Freya never gave up on us. She always loved me, even when I did the unthinkable and shattered her heart. Her grey eyes glassed over as the tears threatened to leave. My throat tightened, my eyes stinging. I was under her spell and had no control. Before I could stop it, a single tear fell down my cheek.

"I'm sorry," she whispered as she wiped her eyes.

I scooped her up into an embrace, pulling her into me before covering her mouth with mine. Kissing away the tears, trying to kiss away the pain we both felt over a year ago. I pulled her onto my lap, kissing her as if she was the only way I could still get oxygen. She was my reason for existence. I reluctantly pulled away, and she whimpered as she lost my contact.

I wiped her tears away with my thumbs. "I shouldn't have driven away. I should have been more determined. I knew where you lived, where you worked, yet I hid behind a phone." I choked. "Freya, this is it. Me and you. No fucking up this time." I sighed. I kissed her once more. "I love you so much," I said, my lips still on hers before kissing her again.

"I love you too." She smiled against my mouth.

"Come on, let's go to bed. I'm exhausted," I said, lifting her off of my lap then taking her hand and leading her to the bedroom.

***

A few weeks had passed, and Freya was finally living with me. I couldn't quite believe it, but I was the happiest man alive.

I had a few errands to run that morning. I showered quickly, pulling a navy suit on and pressing my lips into her hair, saying goodbye. She normally stirred when I kissed her, but she was in such a deep sleep. I opened the bedside table and pulled out a piece of paper.

'I did kiss you goodbye, but you were too busy snoring – Love C x'

I smiled and let out a little chuckle as I placed the note on the pillow. James was waiting for me.

"Morning, boss." He smiled as he opened the door for

me. "Morning, James," I said before sliding in the back. I didn't have to tell him where we were going. I had spoken to him a couple of weeks ago about this. My work schedule had been crazy, and this was the first break I'd had. I tapped a number into my phone and listened to it ring before I heard his voice.

"Hello," he said sternly.

"Harry, it's Carter." I heard the exasperated sigh that left his mouth.

"Carter," he said, unimpressed.

"Harry, I am calling to apologise for how poorly I treated your daughter. I know you know we're back together. I will forever be dampened with guilt from what I did to her. We have spoken, we have forgiven, and we have moved on. But, I do call for a reason," I said, nervous.

"Go on…" he said, not letting up his tone.

"I want to ask for Freya's hand in marriage on Christmas Day. But of course, unless I have your blessing, I won't do it," I said quietly, begging for his blessing.

"Carter, how can I deprive my daughter of the man she loves? I will forgive you, but in time. But yes, I do give you my blessing as long as you promise to love and cherish her for every single living day that you breathe. You are to never hurt her and always protect her, do you understand?" he said sternly.

"Of course. I would never dream of hurting her again. She is my everything. My reason for existence. Thank you,

Harry. I'm on the way to get the ring now," I said, smiling when I could hear Rose talking in the background.

"Rose has just asked if you got her message about her ring size."

"Yup, I got it. Tell her thank you."

We said our goodbyes just as we pulled up outside Cartier. This was it. I couldn't wait to ask her to be my wife.

I walked into the lavish store to be greeted by a lady called Vivienne. She smiled warmly at me as she walked me through to a private office at the back of the store.

"Morning, Mr Cole," she said as she showed me to my seat before sitting down.

"Morning," I replied.

"I have been speaking to you on the phone, going through the designs with you. Thank you for coming in so promptly. We didn't think it would be back just yet, but it came in late last night. Do you wish to see it?" she asked as she unlocked a small safe behind her.

"Of course" I nodded. I felt so nervous. I knew in my head what it looked like but nothing could compare to what I felt when I saw it. She closed the safe behind her and handed me the red velvet box.

I opened it slowly, my mouth dropping when I saw just how beautiful it was. A four-carat, tear drop shaped diamond that sat on a thick platinum band, with small encrusted diamonds either side of the main diamond. It was perfect for

her.

"It's perfect. Thank you, Vivienne." I smiled. She took it back from me, her hands covered by the gloves as she polished it up again and placed it back into its box.

I pulled out my wallet and handed over my bank card as she took the payment. After a few minutes, she gave me the box and congratulated me once more. I thanked her and put the box safely into my pocket. I took my receipt then walked out to the kerb where James was waiting. I wasn't going back into work today. I decided to work from home. I wanted to make sure everything was ready and sorted for the proposal. Christmas was fast approaching, and I wanted to make sure everything was perfect. As we drove back towards the penthouse, I pulled my phone out and tapped a message to Freya.

'Hurry home Miss Greene, I miss you X'

I had just sat down at my laptop to work when my phone rang. It wasn't a number I recognised.

"Hello?" I said.

"Hello, Mr. Cole. It's Jason from security at Lornes & Hucks. I've been asked by Miss Greene to contact you. She is unwell. She has asked if you could get here as soon as possible."

I was already on my way to the car by the time he finished his sentence. "James!" I shouted as I rushed to the lift. James followed me.

"I'm on my way," I said abruptly before cutting off the phone.

I pushed the pedal to the metal and floored it out of the car park, cutting through the London traffic like a mad man to get to her. I abandoned the car outside and left James as I ran into her building. I headed towards the front desk.

"Where is she?" I asked the petite blonde lady behind the desk. She stood and pointed down the long corridor. I ran again and pushed the ladies' toilet door so hard it smacked against the wall and sprang back. "Freya!" I called, my voice frantic with worry. I stuck my head around the corner cubicle and found her cradling the dirty toilet bowl. Her eyes were red raw from where she had been crying. "Oh, baby." I knelt down beside her, kissing her clammy forehead. "Let's get you home."

I scooped her up as if she was as light as a feather, flinging her bag over my shoulder. She clung onto my shirt as I walked towards the lobby, thanking the security guard and receptionist before walking outside into the cold air. I was thankful to see James had the door open ready for us. I placed her gently on the back seat, pushing her across slightly so I could scoot in next to her.

"Are you okay?" I asked, brows furrowed, knowing full well she wasn't okay.

"No." she wailed.

"Is it a bug?"

"I think so. It's been going round the office and now I've been struck with it," she cried.

I had already text Julia to ask her to run a hot bath for Freya.

"Julia has run you a bath. Once you're done, straight to bed," I said sternly.

I was relieved when we pulled up at home. She had paled again, her skin clammy. She tried to walk, but I wouldn't allow it. I picked her up and walked her into our bathroom, placing her down in front of me. She was so frail. I slowly undressed her before taking her hand to support her as she stepped into the hot bubble bath. I took off my t-shirt off. I could see her big grey eyes devouring me.

"I don't think so." I grinned as her.

She sulked as she slid down into the bath so her hair was under the water. I knelt down beside the bath, foaming my hands with soap before lathering her up, feeling her tensed muscles slowly relax. I reached into the bathroom cabinet, grabbing a small jug, filling it up with water and pouring it over her body to wash away the soap suds. She gave me a cute smile. "Thank you," she said.

"You're most welcome" I kissed her the cheek before lifting her out of the bath.

I laid her down in our huge bed, tucking her in. She looked so beautiful in her silk nightie. She snuggled down under the duvet and put *Friends* on. I lay next to her, on top of the duvet, replying to my work emails. I didn't want to work, but Freya told me she was fine. So I compromised by working next to her. That way I could keep an eye on her.

A couple of hours had passed when she started fidgeting. "Babe," she said quietly.

"What's wrong?" I asked, concerned.

"Nothing. Could I have some toast? I'm so hungry." She gave me her best puppy dog eyes. She had me hook, line, and sinker.

"You're meant to starve a bug." I frowned at her.

"It doesn't feel like a bug. It could have been something I ate. Tom bought some egg and sausage rolls in for breakfast." She knitted her eyebrows together as if she was trying to remember something. "They did taste a bit funny."

"And you still ate it?" I asked, not sure if I was disgusted or frustrated.

"Babe, this is me. I don't turn down food." She elbowed me, giving me her biggest and best grin. "Now, please, some toast with butter," she demanded before shooing me off the bed.

I didn't protest. I got up and rushed down to the kitchen to make her some toast and a cup of tea. I sat on the bed and handed her the plate, her eyes lighting up and her tongue darting out of her mouth to lick her lips. I could hear her tummy grumble. I left her to eat, sitting close to her as I continued to work. I looked up from the screen when I heard Freya's phone beep. She smiled as she opened the message from Courtney. I was glad she was checking in on her.

I heard Freya sigh as she placed her phone on the bedside table. She shifted closer to me and started running her finger slowly up my leg. I knew what she was trying to do. I shook my head, looking at her, and she bit her lip. She ran two fingers up and down my thigh. I was hard from just her touch.

As she reached my groin, she could feel how hard my cock was for her, and she continued to run her fingers over me.

I took a deep breath in. "Freya, you're meant to be resting." I looked down my nose at her.

"But I don't want to rest." She climbed on top of me then picked my laptop off the bed and put it on the floor beside us. As she moved back up, her eyes burned into mine. She needed rest, but I couldn't resist her. I was like a moth to a flame; I just couldn't stay away.

I moved closer to her, kissing her full lips before pulling away and nipping her bottom lip. I continued trailing soft kisses down her neck and towards her collarbone, occasionally nipping her skin. I tucked my little finger under the spaghetti straps of her black, silk nightie, pulling them down her arms delicately. I took one of her breasts into my mouth, sucking her nipple hard, causing a gasp to leave her. She was trying to push me away, and greedily trying to pull me free. She was panting and so ready from the little contact we had.

She lifted herself up, as if she was signalling for me to pull my trousers down. I threw my head back in defeat, keeping my eyes on her as I did as she wished. I put my hungry mouth around her pert nipples, sucking and licking as she groaned. I pushed her nightie up around her waist as she lifted slightly, guiding me into her soaked core and began moving her hips slowly.

She was already tightening, her breath quickening. She stopped her thrusts to compose herself then leaned her body down to me, my sage eyes on her hungry grey pools. They almost looked stormy. Her lips hovered over mine, but before she could kiss me, I pushed her off me, pinning her arms above her head with my left hand. With my right hand, I pushed her thighs apart, running two fingers down her centre before slowly plunging them into her while brushing my thumb over her sensitive bud, her moans intoxicating me.

I didn't want her coming on my fingers. I pulled them out before thrusting my hard cock into her. Her moans became louder as I fucked her harder, deeper. My lips were back on her neck, and I breathed in her scent of Chanel No.5 before kissing her as I continued my fast, hard thrusts.

Freya called out my name as she tightened around me.

I leant down and whispered into her ear, "Come."

She clamped down around me, coming hard before pushing me to my own release.

We lay next to each other, panting hard as we came down from our high. I pushed my hand through my hair then leaned on my side, facing her. Her skin glistened with post-sex sweat.

"Now, you nympho. Can I get back to my work?" I smirked.

"Of course." She beamed at me, facing me. "I got what I wanted."

"Well played, Freya," I laughed gently, the smile still on my face. "Now, seriously. Get some rest. You need to get better."

"Fine." She scowled at me. "I'm just going to get some water," she said before slipping out of bed and walking out of the bedroom.

I sat back, resting against the headboard, losing myself in my work when Freya burst through the bedroom door, glowing a crimson red.

"You okay?" I asked. "Are you feeling sick again?" I started to get off the bed.

"No. I, erm, I just bumped into James in the kitchen," she stuttered.

"Lucky James."

"You're not mad?"

"Why would I be mad?" I asked, confused. "You're mine, I'm yours. James and the rest of the household know that so there's nothing to worry about." I patted the bed next to me. "Time for rest."

She lay next to me then leant across and kissed me. "You know how to treat a lady." She winked. "I'm very lucky to have you all to myself."

She bit her lip, rolling over.

I smirked as I watched her perfect arse come into view where her nightie had ridden up slightly. I couldn't help but give it a soft slap.

CHAPTER FIFTEEN

I woke warm and content. Once my eyes adjusted, I could see my Freya lying there, eyes pinned to the ceiling, as if she was in a daydream.

"Morning, beautiful." I smiled and kissed her on the cheek.

"Morning, handsome." She smiled back at me as she received my kiss.

"Sleep well?"

"Like a log." She beamed at me.

"You feeling better? You look a little washed out. Have you been sick again?" I asked, concerned.

"I have," she said quietly, her eyes flitting. She was struggling to look me in the eyes.

"Oh, baby," I said sympathetically. "I hate that you're ill." I leaned across, kissing her forehead. "Hopefully the bug will be out of your system soon." I rolled onto my back, rubbing my eyes.

"I don't think it's a bug," she whispered. Her voice

quivered as if she was trying not to cry.

"What do you mean?" I sat up, cocking my head to the side as my eyes searched her face. She didn't look up at me.

"I've skipped my period," she muttered, "I don't know how. I'm on the pill. I haven't skipped any. I take it at the same time every. Single. Day." She emphasized the last three words. She threw her head back as tears escaped her, running down her cheeks.

My heart was pounding so hard, I could hear it in my ears. Pregnant? I tried not to get too excited.

"You've not tested, have you?" I spoke quietly, trying to keep my voice calm.

"No." She continued to sob.

"Then don't worry yet. It could just be stress. I will send James out to grab a couple of tests. Please don't get upset. We can deal with it." I smiled softly, kissing away her tears.

She smiled at me. "You are wonderful," she said, grabbing my hands and squeezing it tight.

"As are you." I squeezed her hand back as I got up. "I'm going to see James. You stay there. Try and rest." I smiled as I walked out the door.

Once the door was closed, I had to stop for a moment to breathe. My heart was beating so hard in my chest.

I ran down the stairs, searching the rooms for James, I let out a sigh of relief when I saw him and Julia sitting in the kitchen snug, having a cup of coffee.

"James. Julia." I nodded, my eyes wide.

"Carter?" Julia asked "Is everything okay?"

"Erm, I'm not sure. I'm trying to keep my cool. James, could you please do me a big favour? I know it's early."

"Of course," he said, standing up. He placed his coffee cup down on the table and walked towards me into the open-plan kitchen. "What do you need?"

"A pregnancy test." I looked him dead in the eyes, not wanting to say anymore on the matter.

"Okay, say no more. I'll be back shortly." He nodded before walking towards the front door. I looked at Julia and smiled at her before making two cups of teas.

"Carter," Julia said as she walked towards me. "If you can, make sure Freya uses her first wee of the day. It will be stronger so it should give you a stronger chance of getting a positive." She squeezed my shoulder.

I nodded then walked back up the stairs. I needed to keep calm for Freya. I couldn't let her see me have a wobble.

I opened the bedroom door, walking into the room. "James has just left. He should be back in about ten minutes."

I walked over to my side of the bed and handed Freya her tea.

"Thank you," she said as she accepted.

I sat next to her and rested my hand on her leg. Inside, I was trembling.

"It will be okay, Freya. Whatever the outcome. I promise."

She nodded in agreement.

"You haven't been to the toilet yet, have you? Only Julia said it's better with the first wee of the morning."

"Okay," she said, taking a sip of her tea and sitting back against the headboard.

We didn't talk, we just sat in silence, waiting for James. I didn't let go of her hand. I wouldn't.

I was getting frustrated. Twenty minutes had passed since I'd sent James to get the pregnancy test when there was a knock at the bedroom door. *Finally.*

I jumped up and jogged to the bedroom door, opening it slightly and taking the bag from James.

"Thank you for that, James." I nodded then closed the door. I reached into the bag and put both pregnancy tests on the bed. "Come on. Let's go find out," I said, hopeful as I walked into our bathroom, Freya following.

I opened the box, pulling out the test and then the instructions, holding the test up in one hand while reading what to do.

"Give it to me." She shook her head as she took the test from me. She took it out of its wrapper then sat on the toilet. "I can't wee with you here," she said, embarrassed. "Can you just wait outside the door? Please?"

I didn't want to go outside, but I had to respect her wishes. I nodded and walked just outside the bathroom door. I heard the toilet flush, letting out a small breath before walking into the bathroom again. I walked straight over to her. Her face was riddled with worry. It consumed her. I wrapped my arms around her as she wound her arms around my waist, squeezing me slightly as she rested her head on my chest. I tried my hardest to slow my heartbeat down so she didn't hear it, but I couldn't. It was thumping so fast and hard in my chest, I didn't know how it was still inside my ribcage.

"Can we look yet?" I asked.

"It says wait three minutes," she said quietly, clinging to me.

"Well, there is something on there already," I said, peeling her scared frame away from my waist. I took her hand as we walked over. As she gasped, I squeezed her hand. There it was; a dark blue cross.

She was pregnant.

She dropped my hand and held onto the sink. She sobbed quietly. *Oh, my darling.*

She didn't need to cry. She didn't need to be scared. I wasn't going anywhere. She was my everything, and so was this baby. This was meant to happen.

I walked close behind her, wrapping my arms around her again, my hands resting on her stomach. I instantly felt protective of her, even more so now as I knew she was carrying my baby.

She looked up at me in the mirror, her eyes trying to

read my expression. Her eyes were red, her skin pale.

"Baby, I promise we will get through this. Everything happens for a reason, remember?" She just stared at me. "We both wanted kids. We want to be together, and we love each other. We will just have another little person to focus on." I swallowed. "Honestly, this is the best news for me. I couldn't imagine not having kids with you. Yeah, okay, it happened a little earlier than we would have liked. But it's happened. We are going to be parents, Freya. I love you." I turned her around and embraced her.

"I'm scared," she whispered through sobs.

"I know you are, and so am I," I whispered back. "But we will be just fine, you know that, don't you?" She nodded. "I promise you, Freya. We will." I cradled her face, kissing her as softly as I could.

She kissed me back, more forcefully, as if she was trying to show me how scared she was, how emotional she felt. She wanted me to feel everything she was feeling.

"Let's keep it quiet until we've had our scan. I'll call my doctor and get us booked in." I smiled. "I am so happy, baby." I rested my hand on her face as she leaned into it, resting her hand on top of mine.

"I love you," she whispered, tears threatening to run again.

I scooped her up and kissed her, taking her mind off of everything for a split second before walking her back into the bedroom. I put her back into bed and put the telly on for her

"I'm going to make you some breakfast. I'll be back soon." I winked at her.

Once I was out the door, I stood at the top of the stairs, trying to let everything sink in. I was going to be a daddy. Freya was going to be a mummy. We were going to be parents to the most amazing little bundle. I didn't know I could love Freya any more than I already did, but since finding this out, I loved her more fiercely than ever.

I made Freya a quick ham and cheese omelette then chose some strawberries, blueberries, and melon, placing them in a bowl. I added a glass of cold, fresh orange juice to the tray. I didn't know what she would fancy, and I wanted to try and keep her sickness at bay as it must have been exhausting for her. I just wanted her to eat. It wasn't just about her anymore.

I placed the tray on Freya's lap, her eyes lighting up when she looked at the tray of goodies. She went straight for the fruit bowl.

"Looks delicious," she said with a mouthful of fruit.

"Now we need to make sure you're eating during the day. It's not just you now," I said, lying on my belly and resting my head on my hands. I stayed in the same position, watching her as she ate. I frowned when I saw her push the tray away. "Freya, you've left half your omelette."

"I'm full up. My tummy has probably shrunk from being sick." She frowned back at me.

I couldn't win this argument. I didn't want to win this argument. "Fine." I huffed, pushing her back so she was propped up against the headboard. I turned on my side and laid my ear on her tummy, looking at her the whole time. I was so happy. I couldn't even contain my happiness. We must have lay like this for at least an hour until she moaned because we had to go and get dressed, ready to meet Laura and Tyler.

I walked out of the bathroom, running my hand through my hair, creating my tousled look as I finished styling it with wax. I was wearing a grey roll neck jumper, dark blue skinny jeans, chukka boots and a Harrington jacket. I sprayed my aftershave and walked over to my queen, kissing her on the cheek.

"You look as beautiful as ever," I mumbled in her ear as I stood close behind her, wrapping my arms tightly around her waist. I focused on her for a while, taking every inch of her in. Her long, auburn hair was curled. She wore a black casual dress, thick tights, and ankle boots. She looked as beautiful as always. She looked sun-kissed, more so than usual, but I think she was trying to hide the fact that she was so washed out. She had been sick a few more times since breakfast. It was horrible to see. I just wished I could take it away from her.

I nuzzled into her neck, smelling her as she finished putting her earrings in. "You smell divine."

"So do you." She looked over her shoulder at me then kissed me quickly, her bright red lipstick lingering on my lips. "That's a good look for you," she teased.

"Yeah? I might rock this out to lunch. Bring it with you." I winked at her as she giggled. All I could think about was her red lipstick round my cock. "Come on, we're going to be late," I said as I walked over to the bedside unit and slipped my Rolex onto my wrist.

"Okay, okay. I'm ready. Let me just get my bag." She walked out of the dressing room, through the bathroom and into the bedroom. "Right, let's go. Is James driving?"

"Not today, I am." I smiled "I've given James the day off."

"That's nice of you." She smiled back at me.

I took her hand as we walked out of the penthouse. I loved her so much.

We walked into the underground car park towards where I parked my cars. I watched as Freya started walking towards the Maserati, her hand resting on her tummy. I wasn't sure if she was doing it on purpose or accidently. I continued walking, not saying anything as I walked towards the Land Rover Discovery parked next to the Maserati. I unlocked it and looked at her.

"When did you get that?" she asked.

"A few months ago." I smiled smugly. "Good job I did, what with our little arrival coming into the world in a few months." I opened her door, taking her heavy bag from her. What the hell did she have in there? It reminded me of when we went to Elsworth and her bag weighed a ton back then. At least she had an excuse; we were staying for a few days. Today, we were going for lunch. I let out a little laugh before shutting the door on her.

"The car is lovely." She smiled at me as I got into the car, her fingers running over the leather interior.

"I'm glad you like it. It's yours." I looked at her with a massive grin on my face.

"What?" she said, shocked. "Carter – I can't. Don't be silly." She shook her head.

"I ordered it before we went Elsworth…" I stopped talking briefly. I didn't want to go back to that time. Not when we had come so far.

"But…"

Shaking my head. "No buts." I took her hand, bringing it up to my lips then kissing it.

"Let's go see our friends. Love you, Miss Greene." I let go of her hand and started the engine.

"I love you too, Mr Cole."

CHAPTER SIXTEEN

I was glad when we arrived at the restaurant. I felt bad asking Freya to keep our news from Laura and Tyler, but I just wanted us to enjoy it for a moment. I wanted us to tell them when we were ready. We had chosen to meet in a little Italian just outside London. I handed the keys over to the porter and walked into the restaurant. The host showed us to our seats where Laura and Tyler were already sitting. Freya smiled as she saw Laura cradling her small bump. I shook hands with Tyler as Freya and Laura hugged each other tightly.

"Oh my God, Lau. Look at you. You look blooming lovely." Freya beamed. "Pregnancy suits you." She stepped back, admiring her best friend.

"Thank you," Laura replied, blushing. "How are you? I ordered you a glass of wine. I have a non-alcoholic. At least I can feel like I'm drinking." Laura laughed.

"Oh, thanks, hun, but I'm not drinking either," Freya replied. I kept my eyes on her. "I'm getting over a nasty bug so still trying to be careful what I eat and drink." She smiled, then I saw the look on Laura's face. Shit, she was panicking because Freya said about the sickness bug.

"Oh, God, don't panic! I was ill at the beginning of the week. I'm fine now. I just don't want to risk it," she said before sliding into the booth next to me.

We sat in light chatter as the waitress bought our drinks over. I smiled when Freya politely declined her wine and asked for water. Laura had her eyes on her best friend, as if she knew what she was hiding.

I picked up my beer, taking a big mouthful. "Oh, that tastes good," I teased Freya.

"So then," Laura said, clearing her throat. "Did you enjoy your weekend in Paris? I know we touched on it." She smirked.

Ohh, so had Freya been telling her about our weekend? A smile crept onto my face.

"Eventful." Freya laughed. "But so amazing." She beamed at me. "Still not happy that you knew he was going and didn't tell me." She scowled at Laura.

Laura sighed. "Like I said, if I had told you he was going, you never would have gone."

"She is right, Freya. You wouldn't have," Tyler piped up.

"Oh, and Mr Cole, I still can't believe you took a girlfriend with you," Laura said.

I let out a low laugh. "That's right, but she knew what

was going on. Like I said to Freya, she was just a fill gap until I got her back."

Freya rolled her eyes. "Very cocky, aren't you?"

"Very."

"Who made the first move?" Tyler asked, winking at me.

"Of course it was Carter. If he hadn't seen me, I would have run back to my hotel. I didn't want to see him." Freya winced. "As horrible as that sounds."

"Don't worry. I understand." I rubbed the back of her knuckles with my thumb.

"Did you have sex more than once the night you met?" Laura asked boldly.

Freya spat her water out and into her lap. We all laughed as I handed her a tissue.

"That's none of your business," Freya said abruptly as she dabbed her dress with the tissue.

I couldn't help but stir it up. "We totally did. All night long." I chuckled then fist bumped Tyler across the table before breaking into laughs again.

"Ohh, you two." Laura laughed.

"Anyway, enough about that. What are you eating?" Freya asked while Tyler and I were still laughing.

"Well, the baby doesn't like overly greasy food, so I might just go for a Bolognese or something," Laura said, studying the menu.

I saw Freya's face drop, small beads of sweat started

appearing on her brow. She took a sip of water. I started talking to take the attention off her.

"Think I'm going to go for a pizza," I replied.

"Can I share with you? I'm not that hungry," Freya said, but she was clearly lying. She said how hungry she was in the car. She was obviously scared she would be sick in front of Laura and Tyler. I completely understood.

"Of course. You okay?" I asked, Freya's eyes flitting over to Laura and Tyler, making sure the coast was clear. Luckily, they were engrossed in their menus.

She looked back towards me, lowering her voice to a whisper. "Still haven't quite got my appetite back."

"Okay, babe. I won't go for a heavy pizza. Something light." I smiled sympathetically at her.

The waiter arrived to take our order, and Freya sat quietly just sipping her water. We only had to wait about twenty minutes before our food arrived. I cut a few slices of my pizza and placed it on a side plate for Freya. She ate a few mouthfuls then pushed her plate away while everyone else continued to eat.

Laura stopped eating and looked at Freya. "Are you okay? It's unlike you not to eat your food."

"I'm fine. It's just this bug has really taken my appetite away."

"You sure it's a bug?" Laura asked.

My eyes bored into Laura. Freya couldn't crack. I

couldn't let this be on her. Freya went to answer when I interrupted, "She's pregnant."

I heard a clatter which made Freya and me jump.

"Oh. My. God," Laura said as her fork hit her bowl. She stared at Freya. "You're pregnant! How? When?"

Tyler shook his head. "Do you really need to know how? Do you not remember?" He chuckled to himself. "I know you claim to have 'baby brain'." He air quoted 'baby brain' with his fingers. "But surely you haven't forgotten that night?"

Laura ignored him. I could feel the icy tension brewing between us all.

"Why didn't you tell me?" Laura asked.

"That's rich coming from you," Freya sniped at her.

I felt like I had to intervene. I couldn't have these two fall out, not now.

"I told her not to tell anyone. I wanted us to get scanned, then make sure everything was okay after our twelve-week scan, which I'm sure you can understand seeing as you didn't tell Freya until you were four months," I said, a little more bluntly than I intended to.

"Sorry, I'm just shocked. When did you find out?" Laura asked, her eyes still focused on Freya.

Freya sighed. "This morning. We're shocked too, Laura. It's not like we planned this, it just happened. We didn't want this just yet, but we are over the moon." She smiled at me.

"Wow, it happened so quickly," Laura said, stunned. "Tyler and I have been trying for about a year, even before the wedding." She looked down, picked her fork up and started twirling her pasta. Tyler reached over and touched her hand, reassuring her, I assumed. "Congratulations, though. It's wonderful. At least our babies will be close," Laura said, a half smile gracing her face. I couldn't work out if she was just saying congratulations or whether she actually meant it.

"That's true. They could be besties, like us." Freya reached across and took Laura's other hand, rubbing it. She was such a caring and sensitive soul. Within seconds, Laura slipped her hand out from under Freya and Tyler's clasp and held her glass up.

"To Freya and Carter." She smiled. We all clinked our glasses and took a sip before sitting in an awkward silence.

We asked our server for the bill as Freya and Laura started chatting.

"It was lovely seeing you both," Freya said. "You will have to come over to the apartment. We're going to start house hunting soon. We want to move out of the city."

"That would be lovely," Laura replied. "Sorry. Please don't think I'm unhappy for you both. It's just a shock. We went through so much to fall, and you know, it's always hard when people fall so quickly and naturally." She started to cry. "Bloody hormones." Laura sobbed into her tissue.

Freya quickly slid out of the booth, wrapping her arms around Laura then kissing her on the forehead. "I know, sweetie. I can't imagine what that must be like."

My heart hurt for them both, I felt for Laura, but I also felt for my darling Freya who couldn't enjoy her moment. The server appeared at the table with the bill. I quickly took it from his hand before Tyler got a chance to grab it then handed the server my card.

"Thank you, Carter. You didn't have to, man," he said as he started to slide out the table.

"Not a problem, mate. It's been lovely." I took my receipt from the guy then slid out of the booth myself.

"I'm sorry about Laura," Tyler said with grimace as he started to walk beside me and behind the girls.

"Don't worry about it. It's clear she's very hormonal. I know she doesn't mean anything by it and that once it sinks in, she will be over the moon." I smiled at Tyler.

"She really will. It's just been so hard. I don't think she has been coping the best, to be honest, so I'm glad that she's had a few hours with Freya. She misses her terribly at work." He sighed.

"I bet. Between me and you, I am trying to get her out of Morgan's grip and back working for me. She is too talented to be working for him," I scoffed.

"True that, my friend. True that," Tyler agreed.

The cold air hit us as we walked outside. I saw Freya shiver slightly. She and Laura were standing next to each other in a huddle.

"Are you okay?" she asked Laura.

"I'm fine. I'm sorry for my outburst. I really am so happy for you and Carter." Laura smiled weakly at Freya. I wasn't convinced.

"I know you are," Freya said before hugging her, then she kissed Laura on the cheek.

The valet arrived, so I handed my ticket over, as did Tyler. The wait wasn't long at all when I saw the car drive round. I couldn't wait to get Freya out of the cold.

We all said goodbye before Freya and I scuttled into our grey car. I blasted the heating and clicked our heated seats on. I let out a shudder before putting my seat belt on.

"Well, that was eventful," I said, raising my eyebrows.

"I know. I feel awful," she admitted as she strapped herself in.

"Why?" I asked, confused as to why she felt like this.

"I didn't know they had such a hard time conceiving. She never said anything."

"Maybe she didn't want to. Maybe she felt she could deal with it on her own."

"Maybe." She nodded before shrugging her shoulders, "I just feel guilty."

"Don't feel guilty. We are as blessed to have this baby as they are," I said before pulling away.

"I know we are, but you know what I'm like."

"You are too caring," I said.

"Thank you for lunch."

"You don't have to thank me. It's your money too."

"It isn't really. We aren't married." She let out a little laugh.

"But we will be." I winked at her. If only she knew that in a matter of a few weeks, she would be my fiancée. "You'll be mine legally."

"I can't wait." She beamed.

"Oh, I've had an email from Dr Cox." I couldn't believe I had forgotten. I blamed the lunch drama. "We're booked in tomorrow, just to have a scan and some blood tests, then they will book our twelve-week scan in."

I was so excited. I couldn't wait to find out our due date. I wanted to skip forward to when the baby was born. If you had said two years ago I would be in a serious relationship, about to be engaged and due to become a father, I would have told you to fuck off. But this was the here and now. I was in a serious relationship with someone I loved so deeply, a connection like no other. Life couldn't get much better than this.

CHAPTER SEVENTEEN

Freya was exhausted, and to be honest, so was I. This day had been such a rollercoaster of emotions. As we walked into the room, she dumped her bag on the chair in the corner and flopped down on the bed. "I'm tired." She yawned.

"How about a nice film tonight?" I asked.

"Oh, I would like that. My choice though." She smiled up at me.

"Of course." I leaned down and kissed her nose. "Do you want me to get Julia to cook you anything? You've barely eaten today, and everything you have eaten, you've thrown back up again."

"I'm okay at the moment. I need to get out of these clothes though." She groaned as she stood up. I sat on the edge of the bed, bending down and undoing my chukka boots. It was good to have them off. As I sat back up, I saw Freya walking towards me before pushing my knees apart and standing in between them. She had a wicked grin on her face. She lifted her dress over her head. She was wearing a silk, black bra. She slowly slipped her tights down her legs then threw them over to where she discarded her boots. She had matching silky panties on. She looked phenomenal.

"Oh, Freya. You are such a dream." I ran my hands down the side of her curvaceous body then pulled her on top of me, both of us falling back into the bed. She leaned into me, kissing me. She was hungry for me; I could see the fire burning in her eyes. She grabbed my Harrington jacket and started pulling it off as if she physically couldn't wait another minute. I pushed her away slightly as I took my jacket and jumper off then pulled her back into me. Our bodies were flush with each other. She slowly teased me with her tongue then devoured me in a kiss. She pushed her hands into my hair, pulling gently as she continued to push her tongue deeper into my mouth, exploring every bit. I rolled her over delicately so I was on top of her. I wanted to take full control. I kneeled up on the bed and undid my belt and jeans, pulling them down. She sat marvelling me.

Once I was just in my boxers, I leant down and covered her mouth with mine once more. My hand ran down the side of her body, slowly teasing her. Her breath hitched.

I stroked my finger across her knickers before pulling them to the side and exposing her. I ran my finger down her centre and grinned as I felt how ready she was for me. I pulled my boxers down then lined the tip of my hard cock at her soaked opening before slowly pushing myself into her. She moaned as she took me.

This felt so much more intimate than it had in weeks. I could feel her clamping down around me already. She was close.

I continued to thrust into her slowly, teasing her and pushing her closer to her orgasm.

I didn't need to pick up the pace, nor did I want to. This felt amazing. She felt amazing. My hand was near her face, the other propping me up as I kept my eyes on her as I continued my slow pushes into her.

"Carter," she moaned into my ear. "I'm going to come."

Fuck, she was stunning. I sped up slightly, continuing my rhythm as she moaned as her orgasm sliced through her body while I emptied myself inside of her, kissing her as if my life depended on it.

I rolled off her in a post-sex coma. She made me shudder, but in a good way.

I turned the telly on while Freya walked into the bathroom for a shower. About ten minutes after, she walked back into the bedroom, a messy bun on her head, wearing a *Friends* t-shirt and baggy pyjama bottoms.

"Ahem, it's film time," she said cheekily.

"I know. What will it be?" I said as I turned *Kitchen Nightmares* off.

"*Twilight*." She beamed before jumping into bed next to me like an excited schoolgirl.

"Oh, God, no." I shook my head. Wasn't happening. I

didn't want to sit and watch a vampire and a werewolf.

"My choice. Yours tomorrow. Chop chop, put it on," she ordered.

I sighed as I got up and went to the DVD cabinet in the living room. I couldn't believe we were going to be watching this, but it made her happy.

I was back in the bedroom with the DVD, putting it on, side eyeing her the whole time.

"Are you excited?" she teased.

"Oh, yes. Very much so," I said sarcastically.

"Good!"

I climbed back into bed and flicked the telly to the correct channel. She lifted my right arm up and snuggled under it. I wrapped my arm around her tightly, kissing the top of her head.

I was excited for tomorrow. Apprehensive, but excited. I couldn't wait to see our little dot on the screen. She couldn't be that far along. I already had the nursery planned out in my head. But first, we needed to find a new home. This didn't feel like home anymore.

***

The last two months had flown. We had our twelve week scan today and I couldn't wait. I didn't want Freya to go to work, but she told me that she *had* to go as she had deadlines. It was her last day at work before our two weeks off for Christmas break. I normally never take Christmas off, but this year, I was. It was mad to think the last time we saw our little dot that we were only four weeks pregnant. I remembered seeing their little heart beat flickering away so fast on the black and white screen. Nothing can prepare you for seeing your baby on the screen. It's so surreal. But in that moment, my heart exploded with so much love. My love for Freya grew, and my love for our unborn child had also grown.

I looked at my watch, waiting to Freya. I stood in the lobby, tapping my impatient foot when I saw her. She was glowing. Her hair was shiny, her eyes glistening. I couldn't stop my smile from spreading when I saw her.

"Ready?" I asked.

"I'm so excited." She kissed me on the cheek.

"Me too, baby. Me too."

The drive to the hospital wasn't too bad. I thought the traffic would be worse, but I was grateful that we arrived with plenty of time to spare. I could sense she was nervous. I was nervous too, but I didn't want to let her know that.

When we got into the ultrasound department, Freya told me to sit down while she booked us in. She walked back over to me, her fingers knotted together. She sat down next to me, sitting close to me before I wrapped my big hands round her little ones.

"I'm starting to get nervous now," she said.

"It'll be fine. I wonder if baby will be born end of June or end of July," I said, trying to keep her mind off of it.

"I think end of June," she chirped. "We will see."

Freya shut her eyes, trying to calm her breathing when Dr Cox came out.

"Miss Greene, Mr Cole. Please come through," he called.

"Here we go," I whispered as I followed her.

"How are you feeling?" Dr Cox asked Freya.

"Okay. A bit crampy but I've heard that's normal?" She smiled at him, but I could see the nerves clear on her beautiful face.

"It certainly is," Dr Cox muttered before jotting down some notes. "Any bleeding?"

"No. None" Freya fiddled with her fingers again. I had come to realise that this was a nervous thing.

"Perfect. Okay, if you would like to lie on the bed for me. Please pull your top up and undo your trouser buttons," Dr Cox said, standing from his desk and walking towards the bed with Freya. He pulled the curtain round, stepping aside. "Once you're ready, call me," he said calmly.

I stood with her as she undid her trousers. I held her arm as she lay down on the bed, her breaths deep as if trying to calm herself.

"I'm ready, Dr Cox," she called out, her voice trembling.

"Please, call me David," he said as he came and sat next to us in front of the ultrasound machine.

"Sorry." She smiled politely at him.

"Okay, this gel I put on is a bit cold, as you know. Sorry," David said.

"It's fine. It's not that cold," she lied.

I could see her heart throbbing in her neck, her breathing fast and harsh while David put the scanner on her belly.

"Okay, let's see your baby!" David said with excitement in his voice.

He pushed the scanner down hard, moving it upwards, downwards, and sideways. He pulled his brows together. Freya was staring at him the whole time.

David let out a deep sigh. "Freya, would you mind going to empty your bladder for me?"

Her eyes shot to mine.

"Is everything okay?" I asked David, worry evident in my voice.

"I'm just finding it hard to get a clear shot of the baby. I think Freya's bladder is too full. It's completely normal so please try not to worry." He nodded at me. But I knew she would be worrying. I was worrying.

I helped her up as she walked out towards the toilet. I let out the breath I had been holding.

"It's fine," David reassured me.

"We just want this so much. We can't help being anxious."

"I completely understand." He nodded at me.

Just at that moment, Freya came back into the room before lying back down on the bed. "Okay, let's try that again, shall we?" He smiled at Freya as he spoke.

A few minutes later, the probe was back on Freya's stomach. We couldn't see the screen yet, but David was clicking and typing. I started to relax, and I felt my shoulders untense.

We were all in silence. Freya was holding my hand so tight my fingers started to go white where the flow of blood was cut off. I watched David take the scanner off Freya's flat tummy and place it back in its holder before swivelling round on his chair. A grimaced look covered his face.

"Freya, Carter. I'm so sorry."

Freya looked at David, her eyes darting back and forth, trying to read his face. I squeezed her hand tightly.

"What's wrong?" Freya asked, her voice tight, I could hear the lump in her throat.

"I'm so sorry, but I can't find the baby's heartbeat," David said quietly.

"Can you check again?" I asked, the tears threatening to leave if I blinked. I couldn't cry. I wouldn't cry not in front of her. I needed to brave, I needed to be strong.

"I can," he said, linking his fingers together. "But your baby is only measuring at nine weeks, when you are actually twelve weeks pregnant, which tells me your baby has stopped growing." David stood up, now moving his eyes to

Freya. "I will give you some time. I'll be back in a few moments," David said with sadness in his voice. He walked out the door, closing it quietly behind him.

As soon as the door was closed, Freya crumbled on the bed. I sat on the edge of the bed, taking her into my arms. I didn't know what to say. I kissed her forehead, my own heart shattering into a thousand pieces. The heart I had spent so long trying to fix, trying to make whole again. Now, I had this gut-wrenching pain in my stomach, and an empty, oozing hole in my heart. I'm in shock that this has happened. Shock that no one told us this was a possibility, and I have an ache thinking that we may never get this again.

I felt her turn her head, looking at the still screen of our tiny baby. Our perfect unborn baby. The tears were brimming. I couldn't hold them back anymore. My tears fell silently, running down my cheeks. The pain in my throat was burning, burning so much I felt like someone had stuck a hot steel pole into my windpipe. Freya gently sobbed in my arms, grief consuming her whole, taking over every inch of her clean soul and good heart. I envisaged a black poison flowing through her veins on its way to her heart to blacken it. Taint it with hurt and grief. Her heart would never be pure again. Like mine. We were both perfectly broken and tainted together.

Doctor Cox entered the room, walking quietly and sheepishly over to us. Freya hadn't moved, my arms still firmly cradling her hollow frame. I felt as if her soul had left, even though she was still there.

"What's the next step?" I asked harshly, my voice betraying me with hoarseness.

"Well, we will send you home for a couple of days. Then you have three options. You can let nature take its course, which can take up to eight weeks. You can have tablets that we insert into your cervix, or you can have the surgery as a day patient. Please do not make any decisions now. Go home and try and enjoy Christmas. I will get Sarah to book you an appointment on the 29th December to come in and discuss your choice. Carter, you have my number. If anything changes in the next forty-eight hours, then please call me." He stepped towards Freya and gave her shoulder a delicate squeeze. "I am so sorry again, Freya."

David turned on his heel and started to walk away before Freya stood up, sniffing and holding her tummy as she did. "David? Can I ask you a question?"

"Of course," he replied.

I was confused, wondering what was about to come out of her mouth.

"I thought that if you had a miscarriage that you bleed and have excruciating cramps." She sniffed again, and right there was a rusty knife piercing and twisting deep within my heart. "That's what my midwife told me. She said I would know if I miscarried." Her voice broke, but she was trying to be strong.

David sighed and faced her. "Freya, you've had a missed-miscarriage. Your baby's heart stopped beating but didn't leave your uterus." He looked down at Freya sympathetically. She looked so small.

"What wasn't I told this? Why haven't I been told about this type of miscarriage?" she spat.

"I don't know. You should have been. I'm sorry, Freya, but I really have to go," he said awkwardly.

I was now angry, my blood boiling. I wanted to shoot up and put my hand round his throat so tight, ramming him up against a wall. But what good would it do? Nothing would change the situation. Nothing was going to bring our angel back. And I feared I had lost Freya.

As Dr Cox walked out of the room, Freya dropped to the floor and let out a heart-breaking scream that turned into choked sobs. The pain she had been holding in this whole time. I ran over, kneeling on the floor beside her, pulling her in and holding her tight, kissing her hair. I sniffed and choked my own tears back.

"Everything will be okay. It will be okay," I said, crying into her hair. We were both consumed in this black hole as we sat crying, only our grief-sodden sobs to be heard.

It took some deep inner strength to get us both off the floor. I stood, wobbly on my own legs as I scooped her up. Her eyes were red raw from the tears, her make-up stained down her perfectly beautiful face. She clung to me like a small, scared child who needed someone to guard her. I was numb, so she must have been frozen. She had to go through this. I was the outsider, merely the spectator in this nightmare. I would do anything to switch places with her. Anything.

CHAPTER EIGHTEEN

I walked us through the front door, putting Freya down delicately as she walked in a trance straight past her mum and dad, straight past Mum and Ava before walking up the stairs. They just stared at me, completely and utterly confused by what was happening. Their smiles faded more and more as she disappeared farther out of sight.

"We've lost the baby," I said, sadness clear in my voice. "There was no heartbeat."

Mum and Ava came and hugged me. Rose stood beside me and leant into me while Harry gave me a gentle squeeze on the shoulder. I looked out of the huddle to see Rose walking upstairs to Freya, Harry following. I pulled out of my family squeeze and tiptoed up the stairs. I needed to see she was okay. I stopped at our bedroom door, my heart breaking more when I heard her.

"I don't want to forget the baby, Mum," I heard her cry. I clutched my chest, the pain searing through me like a knife.

"Oh, sweetie. You will never forget. I still think of our

three..." I heard Rose say before I decided to step away. I didn't want to eavesdrop on a private conversation. I had to remember to call the decorators. We hadn't told anyone yet but we had bought a house in Surrey, our family home. I got too excited and had them start on our nursery. I couldn't let Freya sort that. I couldn't let her see it. I heard silence and movement, so I stood back outside the bedroom door, Freya's eyes finding mine. I always felt her presence. I always wondered if she felt mine. We were connected. Our souls entwined.

"Ah, okay," Rose said. "We will go unpack and get settled. We'll leave you to it." She kissed Freya on the forehead and wiped a stray tear from her eye before walking towards me.

"Love you, baby face," her dad said before getting up off the bed and following Rose. I smiled at them both as they passed me, Harry patted my chest before closing the door behind him. I looked over at her, a ghost sitting there. Hollow and afraid. Broken and tormented with grief. Completely overcome with loss.

"Hey, beautiful." I kissed her forehead.

"Hey." She leaned up and kissed me on the lips. "You okay?"

"Not really. I can't stop thinking about it." I sighed. "I can't stop thinking about you."

"I'll be okay. We will get through this," she said, standing up slowly. "Come on. It is Christmas, after all."

I was in awe. The strength of this woman was like no other. I fell more in love with her each day. I stood up with her, scooping her into an embrace and kissing her deeply. I poured all of my love and emotions into this one kiss. Her arms linked round my neck, giving me the contact I always craved. I pulled away, my eyes burning into hers. I felt like I could see deep into her soul, feeling everything she was feeling. I pecked her lips one last time before we went downstairs.

We ordered a Chinese. We were going to cook, but after everything that had happened, we just wanted to try and rest and enjoy our evening as much as we could. I took a breath, pushing back on my chair then rising to my feet, clearing my throat.

"Freya and I would like to thank you for coming and spending Christmas with us. Even though we've had this heart-breaking news today, we really wouldn't want to spend our Christmas any other way. So, thank you for spending it with us," I toasted.

Everyone held up their glasses of wine and clinked.

Once dinner was done, my mum and Rose tidied up. Freya nipped upstairs to get changed. After ten minutes, she came and found me on the sofa and leaned into me. I wrapped my arm around her and pulled her in as close as I physically could.

"I can't wait to see the new house again. Fresh start," she whispered to me, smiling.

"I know. Me too," I said, my hand moving round to her tummy. We were interrupted by my mum and Rose plonking themselves down next to us.

"How are you feeling, dear? I know that's a silly question," my mum said, eyeing me up. She knew how my temper could rise quickly.

"Don't be silly," she said, still snuggled into me, a smile gracing her face. Fuck, it was good to see her smile. "I'm not bad, thank you. Looking forward to Christmas. We can deal with all of this after." Again, she knocked me. She was such a dream.

"We will make it such a wonderful Christmas, all of us here together," my mum said.

"That we will," Rose added.

I sat just listening. I hadn't felt like speaking much. I think it was finally hitting me. Hitting me that we had lost our baby. Sadness consumed me, but I didn't feel like I could grieve because I needed to be there for Freya. Freya needed to be sad; it was her that was going through all of this. I was merely looking in on the situation.

I was brought back from my daze when I felt a pulse of electric course through me. Freya's hand was finding its way inside mine, giving it a squeeze. I tried to blink away the tears, swallowing to push the lump back down my throat, then smiled at her.

"Why don't you tell our mums about our new house?" she suggested.

My eyes glazed over, looking at her. I had a new level of admiration for her. I then glanced over at my mum and hers. "Oh, yeah." I coughed. "Of course. We've bought a house in Surrey. That way, the commute isn't too bad for Freya and me. It's a beautiful detached house on one and a half acres of land." I smiled at her. "It's six bedrooms, has a swimming pool, study, gym, and a guest house which has three bedrooms, a kitchen, and a lounge so my wonderful housekeepers have their own space. Plus, enough room for all of you. We should be moving in January." I lifted Freya's hand up to my mouth, bringing it to my lips and kissing it softly.

"It sounds lovely, sweetie," my mum said. "What will you do with this place?"

"I'm not sure yet. We might keep it." I shrugged. "Haven't thought that far ahead."

"Well, I think it sounds wonderful. I can't wait to see it," Rose said.

"Hey, would you mind if I went to bed?" Freya asked quietly. "I'm exhausted. It's been such a long day and, to be honest, I'm emotionally drained."

"Of course, darling." Rose stood up with Freya and cuddled her, then pecked her on the cheek. My mum waited her turn for her cuddle and kiss. She waved goodnight to Ava before being embraced by her dad, giving her a squeeze. I

174

could see the pain etched on his face. I couldn't imagine how it felt to see your daughter so broken. And then I remembered, this wasn't the first time he had seen it. The first time was because of me.

"Night, baby face." He smiled at her. She looked behind, her eyes searching for mine when I mouthed that I would be up shortly.

I needed to get everything sorted for tomorrow.

Once I heard the bedroom door close, I hopped off the sofa. I slipped into my office, pulling the drawer open checking that the ring was still there. I let out a sigh of relief. I panicked constantly, thinking I would lose it. I closed the drawer and walked back into the lounge area. My mum, Ava, and Freya's parents knew to hide in the morning. I wanted this moment to be just about me and Freya. I originally planned to do it on Christmas Day, but I felt like now was the right time to do it. I went into the pantry and looked at the stockpiles of LED candles and the boxes of red roses. I couldn't see the floor due to the amount of roses. For the first time that day, a small bolt of happiness shot through me. I wished my parents goodnight before I started grabbing the boxes of roses, and I began placing them at the edge of the staircase. After an hour of layering up the staircase, I collected the LED candles and placed them strategically in-between the roses. Another hour had passed, and I was done. I stepped back for a moment to admire my work. I couldn't wait to see her face when she was standing at the top of the staircase, the LED candles reflecting off the glass balustrades. My heart swelled.

I looked at the time. It had already gone one a.m. I stretched, reaching up to the ceiling. I left the candles on and made my way upstairs to bed. I stripped off as soon as I got into the bedroom and climbed into bed behind my darling, wrapping my arms around her. I nuzzled my face into her auburn hair before succumbing to sleep.

Noise woke me from my sleep, and I looked in the bed next to me, Freya wasn't there. Oh, shit. Don't tell me she went downstairs for water. Fuck. I hopped out of bed and walked towards the bedroom door when I heard a noise behind me. I turned and saw her standing by the window, her arms wrapped around herself. I was behind her within seconds, wrapping my arms around her, pressing my lips to her neck.

"Come back to bed, baby," I said sleepily.

"I can't settle. I've had the worse night," she mumbled, facing me.

"Please, come." There was a twitch on my lips as I ushered her back to bed, lying behind her once more, pecking her on the neck. "Love you."

"I love you too."

I stroked her hair, trying to get her to relax. I felt her

get heavy in my arms, her breathing calming. Then she was gone.

"Night, my queen. Our tomorrow starts today," I whispered.

I woke early, threw on my jeans and a t-shirt. I went downstairs then started ushering my mum, Ava, and Freya's parents into the kitchen. I re-arranged the roses. My heart was thumping. I looked towards the stairs when I heard a noise, smiling as I saw her. Her eyes were still puffy from sleep, her auburn hair messy from the bed. But she still looked fucking amazing. Her eyes darted around, looking at the roses and candles. Tears welled in her eyes.

I stood at the bottom of the stairs, looking up at her. "You coming down?" I asked, still beaming at her. I watched as she walked slowly down the stairs, her hand running down the oak bannister as she did. Her eyes stayed on mine the whole time. I held my hand out for her as she touched the bottom step.

"What's all this? Where is everyone?" she asked, her voice shaking.

"They're out picking up some last minute bits for Christmas." I smiled, knowing full well they were sitting in the kitchen.

I took both her hands in mine, running my thumbs across the back of her knuckles. "Freya," I choked, my voice betraying me. I was cursing internally.

"I love you so much. I honestly have never, ever felt like I do with you." I smiled once more. "After everything that has happened, well, I just love you even more." Her eyes were so wide, I could have lost myself in them.

"This was always my plan, just not with these circumstances." I looked deep into her grey pools. She watched me eagerly, guessing my next move. I took her left hand, slowly dropping down onto one knee. "Please would you do me the extraordinary honour of becoming my wife?"

Yes, I used a similar line out of *Twilight*; I knew it was one of her favourites. Plus, everyone loved Edward. I held out the stunning ring I picked out for her. My heart was beating loud in my chest, the blood pumping to my ears.

I felt like I was waiting forever, but I knew it had been seconds. I smirked when the tears started pricking in her eyes. I already had her answer, but I wanted to hear the sweet three letter word slip off her tongue.

"Yes! Of course, yes!" she exclaimed. I pushed the ring onto her finger, my smile so big it was like I had slept with a coat hanger in my mouth.

I scooped her up, spinning her around as I kissed her passionately. The heat was building. If there was no one else in the house, I would've taken her right there and then on the stairs. I could feel the heat penetrating from her; she felt the same. Her hands dug in my hair, tugging it as she continued wrapping her tongue round mine. She pulled away, frozen when her parents and my mum and Ava came around the door, squealing with excitement as everyone rushed over to congratulate us. Oh, it was wonderful seeing the smile on her face. She was truly stunning.

CHAPTER NINETEEN

I walked into the bedroom to find Freya crying.

"Hey," I said, low and soft. "Are you okay?"

"Mm, just thinking." She smiled, her eyes still filled with tears.

"About what?" I asked.

"Everything. Our baby. Our engagement. Us." She looked at me and took my hand.

"We will get through this. I've been thinking this little bundle in here," I said, pointing at her belly, "has been sent to us for a reason, and even though we don't know what that reason is, we will. This baby was just too precious for this world at the moment. They will come back to us. I know it." I leaned down, kissing her forehead, lingering a little longer than usual. The smell of her perfume filled my nostrils. The spark ignited in me from our touch; I would never get sick of this feeling. I moved away slightly. She propped herself up on her elbows and kissed me as if she was going to lose me forever. I put my hands on her face. I slowly kneeled up onto the bed between her legs, hovering over her. I pulled away again, looking at her, and she was looking at me. I smiled at her, about to get up when she grabbed my tee and pulled me back into her, her hungry mouth covering mine. Our kiss was aggressive, pent up emotions taking over. I ran my hand up her top and pulled away from her as I pulled her t-shirt over her head, throwing it on the floor and kissing her lips again, this time a lot softer than before. She lifted the t-shirt over my head, my lips moving down to her neck, a sweet moan leaving her. I covered her mouth with my hand, my lips twitching into a smirk. Fuck, what I would do to fuck her while gagging her. Shit.

"Shh. It's not just us in the house."

She nodded eagerly as I wrapped my fingers under her panties and pulled them off then pulling my trousers down and slowly entering her. Her moans were like ecstasy, spurring me on to push her to her orgasm. We needed this. This connection.

We all sat in the lounge with the fire roaring. Freya was snuggled into me, my fingers running up and down her thigh, in a trance. Christmas Eve was finally upon us and I couldn't have thought of a more perfect way to spend it than this.

"I'm going to call Laura," Freya said out of the blue.

"Okay, baby. Are you going to be okay?" I asked, concerned, I didn't want her getting upset again.

"I need to do it." She nodded, biting her lip. She stood up, pulling her phone out of her back pocket and walking into the bedroom. I followed her, far enough but still close.

Ten minutes had passed when Freya appeared on the landing and I saw her weeping eyes. My darling Freya. I pulled her into me, kissing her. "It's okay baby," I muttered.

It was Christmas morning, and Freya was like an excited schoolgirl. We sat opposite each other and I placed a medium-sized box on her lap, smiling like the Cheshire Cat. She tore the wrapping paper, revealing the iconic green leather box. Her eyes were alight with wonder. Once the wrapping paper was off, she opened the box slowly and gasped to reveal her silver Rolex, encrusted with diamonds round the watch face. She turned it over, reading the engraving on the back. '*Our forever starts today – C x*'.

She kneeled up and threw her arms around me. "Thank you so much. It's beautiful." She kissed me softly on the lips.

"You're more than welcome." She smiled back at me.

"Okay, okay, your turn!" she said excitedly. She handed me a bigger box. I could see she was embarrassed about her wrapping.

I delicately started to unwrap, savouring this moment. This right here had to be one of my favourite moments. Her eyes lit up, excitement on her face. No sadness, no tears. Just perfect her. A smile crept onto my face, growing as I saw the familiar green leather box. I opened the box, the smell hitting me. It was vintage. A stunning watch sitting on a black leather strap. I looked up at her, still smiling when she twirled her finger at me, indicating for me to turn it over. I did as she asked and saw that she had too had it engraved. *'Forever mine, forever yours – F x'.* I leant across, pulling her onto my lap and kissing her. "What a wonderful gift," I said, squeezing her.

"You're welcome. It's hard to buy for someone who has everything." She smiled back at me. My mouth twitched. I loved her so fucking much.

"Come. Let's go have breakfast. I'm hungry," I said.

We walked into the dining room with our family, all sitting and talking about what we were grateful for.

Me? I was grateful for this beautiful woman sitting next to me.

CHAPTER TWENTY

Christmas was soon over; the Christmas blues were in full swing. I felt even worse today. We were back in Dr Cox's office. It was a bittersweet day. On one hand, it was our chance for a new beginning, but on the other, we were still broken. The end of our journey for the moment. I still couldn't quite get my head around it. Why couldn't we have this miracle that was sent to us? I wanted to talk, wanted to ask if she was okay, but I didn't want to bring it up. I knew she wasn't okay. I knew, as sad as it all was, she just wanted this all over. We needed to move on.

We sat in the waiting room, Freya knotting her fingers, nerves ripping through her. We weren't waiting long when Dr Cox called out for us. We followed him into his office. He sat down, Freya sitting down in front of him, me next to her.

"How have you been feeling, Freya?" David asked.

"No different. Still a bit sick here and there, but nothing to be alarmed about, I don't think." A small, innocent smile crept onto her face.

"Okay, that's good. What have you decided?"

"Well, neither of them sound appealing, but I think it will be the surgery. If that's okay." She squeezed my hand and her eyes met mine. I could see the hurt in her eyes. I could see she was screaming out for help. I wanted to tell Cox not to touch her. I didn't want him laying a fucking finger on her. She had had so much hurt the last few days, I just wanted her to be happy. I want all this behind her. I was trying to calm my thinking. I wanted to talk, I wanted to agree with her and tell her I respected her choice. But I couldn't. I couldn't get the words out. My heart was being obliterated minute by minute.

"Of course. If that's what you want. We will do some observations then take you down to have the process started," he said with a grimace. "I will be back in a moment." He got up and left the room, closing the door quietly behind him.

"Are you okay?" she asked me.

"Yeah, sorry. Just don't want you having to go through this." My face slackened; my brow furrowed. My eyes darted about in concern. I just wanted to take her away to hide.

"I'll be fine. We will be able to start again. We both know we want a baby now, so what's stopping us from trying again?" She smiled like the fucking warrior she was.

"Why are you so wonderful?" I asked

"You make me wonderful."

"You're so brave, my love," I said, kissing her.

"I don't feel it. I'm so scared. I don't want to lose this baby. I love it so much already. But, it is what is. We had no control over this outcome." A tear strayed from her crystal grey eyes. Fuck, my heart. I ran my thumb across her cheek, wiping the tear away.

"I love you so much, Freya."

"I love you too."

We were interrupted as Dr Cox walked in. "Okay, we're ready for you, Freya. Carter, if you could sit in the waiting room, we shouldn't be long.' I wanted to scream no. I wanted to go with her, hold her hand throughout it all. I nodded. That was all I could do.

She got up. I stood up with her, scooping her into my arms and kissing her as hard and passionately as I could. I couldn't tell her how I was feeling, but I was hoping I could show her. We pulled away, Freya standing with me, lingering a little longer.

"I'll be waiting for you." I smiled, kissing her on the lips once more.

"See you soon," she mumbled before walking towards the door. "Okay, I'm ready," she said bravely. I could tell she was crying inside. I was crying, my heart shattering into a million pieces.

Once the door was shut, I cried, throwing my head into my arms, finally getting my release that I had been holding in for so long. I didn't want to cry in front of her, I didn't want to break. But there is only so much you can hold in when the woman you love is going through so much and there is nothing you can do for them.

I held a bated breath, my mind in overdrive when I finally heard the door go, Dr Cox walking towards me. I wanted to run to him, but he was already in front of me, his hand on the top of my arm.

"Freya is in recovery. Everything went as well as it could have. We did have a complication, but I will explain once we're all together. You ready?" he asked before walking me towards the recovery room. My throat tightened as I looked at her asleep. I knew she was fine, but seeing her lying there, slowly coming around, was horrible.

"Carter," she murmured.

"Baby, I'm here," I cooed as I sat down in the large, bat-winged leather chair next to the bed. Her smile was heartbreakingly beautiful.

"Freya, Carter." Dr Cox, the bastard, ruined our moment. Her eyes moved to him. I took her hand in mine.

"So, the operation went well, but during the surgery, because we go in blind as such," he said with a grimace, "we can cause damage, and unfortunately we clipped your fallopian tube which could make conceiving harder."

I didn't pull my eyes from her, her grey eyes turning glassy, the sniffs escaping before she broke into choked sobs. I stood up, wrapping my arm around her shoulders and pulling her into me, kissing her hair. I couldn't take any more heartbreak, and neither could she. She was delicate, like a china doll, and I was scared one more thing was going to break her completely and no one, not even me, could piece her back together again.

***

It had been a week since Freya's surgery. Each day she got better, seeing the positives rather than the negatives. Which, once again, I admired. I rolled over in bed, seeing her awake. "Morning, beautiful." I smiled and kissed her, taking in her scent.

"Morning, you." She smiled back, accepting the kiss.

"How are you feeling this morning?" My hand moved to her tummy, slowly running it back and forth.

"A bit better. Not as sore now. Looking forward to getting back to work."

I grunted. I didn't want her going back to work, not now, not never. I wanted her to come back to work with me, so I could keep an eye on her. Not in a stalker way, just in a loving fiancé way. It annoyed me. I didn't want her working for Morgan.

"You still have two weeks off. Doctor's orders." I smirked. I lifted my arm up, inviting her to lie into me. I loved having her close to me.

I loved mornings like this, just lying there. We were going to see our new house today and I couldn't wait. We needed to go and get some measurements and I really didn't want to inconvenience the builders just for measurements. After half an hour of us just festering, she pulled herself from me, whining as she did before padding through to the bathroom for a shower.

After a few moments, I followed her, like the desperate man I was, constantly needing to be near to her. I was never letting her out of my sight again. I saw her standing in the shower, her hand on her belly. A pang of sadness stabbed into me. I just wanted to give her what she so desperately wanted. A baby. My baby.

I stepped in behind her, kissing her neck as soon as we were touching. She spun round to face me, the sadness deep in her eyes. We didn't need to say anything, we just stood there letting the water cascade over us. I kissed her passionately, losing myself in her. I groaned in appreciation as her arms draped round my neck, leaning into me so her naked body was pressed up against me. My cock throbbed. God, I just wanted to bury myself in her, but I couldn't. We had to go to the house. I tightened my arms around her waist, pulling away. Our noses touched as the water dripped down from my hair and onto my nose before landing on her plump lips.

"As much as I would love to stand here all day with you,

we do need to be at the house soon." I smiled.

"You came into my shower, Mr Cole, not the other way round," she pointed out. Fuck. I wished I came in the shower. I wished I'd made her come in the shower.

"I couldn't resist. My mind is going crazy with different scenarios I would rather be doing to you now, but we have to get ready." I smirked, biting my lip, stopping myself covering her mouth with mine.

"Well, I'm done. You still need to actually shower," she said as she stepped out of the shower and walked over to the sink unit before brushing her teeth. Her eyes watched me in the mirror as I washed. She wanted me as much as I wanted her.

I walked into the dressing room to see her dressed in an oversized knitted jumper and jeans. I had my towel wrapped around my waist, her eyes drawing up and down my body.

I decided to play a little game. I dropped my towel to the floor, knowing full well her eyes were on every inch of me. "What to wear, what to wear." I looked over my shoulder and winked at her.

"I would rather you stay like that, if I'm being honest," she said.

I laughed. Cheeky minx.

"Wait 'til later." I smirked again.

I slipped my boxers on then pulled my jeans up and buttoned them then grabbed my cream roll neck and pulled it over my head. I slipped my Rolex on and smiled as she pushed her ring onto her finger before clasping her own Rolex up.

"You excited to see our house?" she asked.

"Yeah, I am. I'm looking forward to getting in there now. Only a few more months." I said before pecking her on the cheek.

"Me too. I can't wait to start afresh. Maybe once we're in there, we can start trying again," she suggested. It shocked me, but in a good way. Fuck, there was nothing more I wanted then to make her a mother to our child.

"That sounds perfect. We can have lots of fun trying." I winked at her, trying to keep the mood light. I held my hand out for her to take, pulling her in front of me

"Oh, I do love you, Mr Cole." She beamed at me, going onto her tiptoes to kiss me. "Ready?"

"After you, beautiful."

She had her hand in mine for the whole journey, not letting go. She needed the reassurance. She wanted the comfort. She didn't want to feel the gaping hole in her heart at our loss. I squeezed her hand as we pulled up to the black gates at the front of the driveway. I pulled the handbrake as I got out of the car, pressing the intercom to open the gates. I jumped back in, smiling as the grand gates slowly swung open into our driveway. I heard her inhale a deep breath as we continued driving up the long driveway. I couldn't contain my excitement when I saw our house as we parked outside. It was a recently re-built modern house, but we still wanted to change a few things as they weren't to my taste. I had to tell them not to continue with the nursery.

We walked up to the front door hand in hand. There were three steps that led up to it. As we opened the double oak doors, there was a large hallway with a staircase in the middle which took us to our landing which led to our six bedrooms. Our kitchen was open-plan; we had black granite work tops and high gloss white kitchen cupboards with a family room overlooking a huge garden. The dining room was off the kitchen and it had a big bay window. I left Freya downstairs while I disappeared to measure some last bits. I walked into our main bedroom to measure for the walk in wardrobes. It took me five minutes. I was wandering down the hallway when I saw the nursery door open. My heart broke as I knew she was in there. Her beautiful face turned towards me, her make-up streaked from her tears. I smiled weakly at her, wrapping my arms around her waist and nuzzling into her hair. My eyes flicked up as I looked at the room; it would have been perfect.

"This room will be used soon, I promise," I whispered before letting go of her, losing that familiar electric charge. "Come on, I'm done. Let's go get some food." I smiled. We walked out of the house, a small smile on Freya's face.

"What do you fancy?" I asked, knowing full well she would jump at the chance of choosing.

"Pizza!" she said enthusiastically.

"Sounds perfect."

We had just pulled up outside the restaurant. I hopped out of the car, closing the door behind me to go round to Freya's side to open the door for her.

"Thank you, but I must admit, James does it so much better." She giggled as she stood close to me before I shut the car door.

I eyeballed her, my eyes boring into hers and my lips twitching before I laughed with her. We walked towards the restaurant as my phone started ringing, I rolled my eyes. Why couldn't I just have one day without the fucking thing going off all the time? As I pulled it out of my jeans pockets, I looked at the caller ID, confused. It was a number I didn't recognise. Freya's eyes were on me.

"Sorry. Let me get this. Hello?" I said.

"May I speak with Carter Cole, please?"

"This is him," I replied.

"I'm a doctor at The London Hospital. I have been made aware that you and Chloe were together a few months back, is that correct?" the stranger asked.

"Yes," I stuttered, confused.

"I am sorry to tell you this, but Chloe unfortunately passed away during childbirth. We need you at the hospital as soon as possible."

"What?" I ran my hand through my hair, my heart thumping. My eyes widened as I was absorbed the stranger's words. Childbirth? She was pregnant?!

My mouth went dry. The stranger was still muttering on the phone, but at that point, I couldn't piece together what was being said.

"Right, okay, we will be right there," I managed to say before cutting the phone off, grabbing Freya's hand, and pulling her back towards the car.

"Carter, what's wrong?" Panic was evident in her voice.

"It's Chloe." I said abruptly. I couldn't stop my thought process. My mouth was working quicker than my brain. I ushered her into the car, slamming the door before running round to my side and starting the engine. I hadn't even done my seat belt as I pushed my foot to the floor, wheel spinning out of the restaurant car park and into the road.

"Oh my God, Carter!" Freya screamed. "Slow down! What the fuck has happened?

"Chloe has died," I said, looking at her.

"She's what?" Freya said in disbelief.

"She passed away during childbirth," I said anxiously. I couldn't fucking believe this. Was the baby mine? How fucked up could this be? I didn't want a baby with Chloe, I wanted a baby with Freya. Only Freya. We were meant to share this moment together, and now it's as if it has been ripped from us once more. I needed to calm down. I had no idea if this baby was mine or whether they were calling me because she had no family. Fuck, Carter. Breathe.

I could feel Freya's eyes on me, beating me down for answers.

"Child birth? Oh my God, Carter! Did you know she was pregnant?!"

Oh, fuck. This looks so bad.

"Of course I didn't, Freya! This is the first I've heard of it!"

"Don't shout at me!" she snapped.

"I didn't mean it. I'm just trying to get my head round this all. I didn't know she was pregnant. She must have been pregnant while we were in Paris. She wasn't even showing. I just can't get my head round it."

She was drinking in Paris. Did she not know? My head hurt; it was fuzzy.

"Carter, calm down. We will sort this. I promise," Freya said calmly, taking my hand in hers, and then running her thumb across the back of my knuckles. I faced her, sheer panic and worry in my eyes. We pulled up outside the hospital. I literally abandoned the car over two parking spaces, Freya jumping out after me and following. I looked behind me, grabbing her hand and pulling her closer to me to keep up. I must have seemed like such a prick to her, dragging her through this. It wasn't fair.

I ran to the reception desk, placing my hands on the top of it.

"Where is Chloe Blackwood? I had a call saying she had given birth," I said. I couldn't control my voice. It was shaking. I felt Freya's presence behind me, pushing herself up close to me to let me know she was there. I took a couple of deep breaths through my nose, trying to calm myself.

"Oh, yes, Mr Cole. Please, level five," the receptionist said, turning back to her computer.

We ran through the corridor. I wasn't wasting time waiting for the lift. I ran the whole five flights of stairs. I got to the top, barging the door in the stairwell open onto the ward floor, my eyes darting up and down the corridor when I noticed Freya wasn't behind me. I looked back to see her panting, gripping her stomach, bent over.

"Freya!" I said as I went to her side. "Oh my God, I'm so sorry. Oh, baby," I said, getting close to her. What a complete cock I was. I was so absorbed in this hell, I forgot about her.

"Are you okay?" I asked. Her eyes speared through me. She was pissed.

"I just need a minute."

I took her hand and slowly walked towards the reception, asking again for Chloe Blackwood. This time, the receptionist nodded then showed us to a side room.

"Please take a seat. The doctor will be in shortly." She shut the door quietly and left us in a dull box room.

"I can't believe this," I mumbled, pacing the room.

"Hey, it will be okay. We will face this together." She

smiled at me, walking towards me before taking my hands and kissing me. I was petrified she was going to leave me after all of this. After everything we had been through, how much more could she take?

Her kiss lingered, growing deeper as our lips locked. I felt as if she was reassuring me, but I didn't know if my mind was playing tricks on me. She pulled away, her hands still holding mine tightly.

"I promise you, Carter. Whatever happens next for us, we will be okay." She placed her hand on the side of my face and looked into my eyes.

I sighed. "I know. I love you."

We were interrupted when a young male doctor entered the room. "Mr Cole?" he asked.

"Yes, that's me."

"Can we talk in private?" The arsehole eyed me. I didn't like him. There was something about him.

"No. This is Freya, my fiancée. What is going on?"

"I'm sorry to say this, but Chloe unfortunately, didn't make it through childbirth. We had no contact details for parents to call so we ran a DNA test on the baby, which is why we contacted you. You are the baby's father."

I felt like the air had been knocked out of my lungs. The room closed in on me. Freya took my hand, holding it as tight as she could. I felt emotionless, empty.

"With that being said, the baby is to go to any living family. Do you have a number for her parents?" the doctor asked.

It took me a moment to register he was talking to me, I just shook my head. "Her dad passed away years ago, and her mum passed away last year. Just before we met. She is an only child as well."

The doctor looked down at his clipboard "Okay, so given the fact that she has no parents, the parental right belongs to you."

I slowly bowed my head. "I didn't even know she was pregnant." Guilt crept up inside me. What a bastard I was. This was karma.

"By the sounds of it, neither did she. She came in with bad cramps. We thought it was her appendix at first." The doctor shuffled on his feet, no remorse in his voice. He was like a robot. "I know it's a lot to take in. Please take a moment. When you're ready, please come and find me." He gave us a weak smile and walked out of the room, the door closing behind us.

I took a step back, falling onto the sofa that was behind me. I threw my head back and put my hands over my face. I fell apart. Every piece of me came undone like a jigsaw puzzle. My Freya, standing in front of me, grieving the loss of her own baby, and there we were, being told that I was a father. A father to a baby I never knew existed. I felt robbed. This wasn't how it was supposed to be. This wasn't the fairy tale. My fairy tale was with Freya. This was all meant to be with Freya. All of our firsts as a couple, and a baby was the one that was ripped from us. I felt her close. She knocked my legs open with hers before standing in between them, looking down on me. I put my arms around her waist and held tightly onto her, my head resting on her chest. The sound of her heart pounding in her chest was somewhat comforting. Her heart that beat for only me. She wrapped her arms around my neck, taking a deep breath. We didn't move. It was like we had been there for hours. She shuffled on her feet, and I kept my arms wrapped round her before standing then taking her face into my hands.

"Please don't leave me." There was desperation in my voice. "I know this wasn't our plan, but this has happened for a reason. I wanted our baby so much. Nothing will ever replace my love for that little one, and I will never stop loving you. I'm scared. I don't think I have ever been so scared, but as long as I have you beside me, I know we will get through this. It's me and you to the end, baby." I kissed her hard, my tongue forcing its way into her mouth, kissing the pain away. I wanted her to feel what I felt. To feel how vulnerable I was feeling. I pulled away, my eyes searching her grey pools.

"I will never leave you. We did it once before and I will never leave you again. No, this wasn't our plan, but this is our new adventure and I'm so glad I get to do this with you. I'm terrified, but I'm not leaving. There's a baby that needs us. I love you so much, Carter." She gave me one more kiss before taking my hand and leading me into the waiting room. My palms were sweaty, my throat tight, my heart racing in my chest. We saw the young doctor walking towards us, holding a tiny bundle. This was the most bittersweet moment for both of us. We were both terrified. I squeezed her hand tightly as the doctor showed us our baby.

My eyes left what was in front of me and found her, my soulmate. My queen. My love. Who, once again, had shown me just how incredible she was. I was forever in her debt. I owed her everything.

She was my life, my love, my Freya.

Forever and Always.

ACKNOWLEDGEMENTS

First of all, thank you to my wonderful husband, who as always, has supported me unconditionally throughout. I couldn't have done this without you.

Lindsey & Nikki, my tribe. My crew. Thank you for listening to me and re-assuring me when I have my moments. I am so grateful for our friendship and bond.

Caz, Yanaira and Anna, thank you for being there for me. You're awesome and I love you all!

Robyn, honestly you have been amazing. Thank you for all of your help and constant support for me and my little books. I am so grateful, thank you for being there and I'm so glad we became friends.

Leanne, my wonderful Leanne. Thank you for making my book and cover look amazing once again and your never ending support.

Karen, thank you for editing my book once again.

I've also made a fan page on Facebook; *Ashlee Rose's Rosie Posies* if you want to come and join.

Instagram: @ashleeroseauthor
twitter: @ashleerauthor

I hope my story gave you a chance to escape the craziness that is happening over the world, thinking of every single one of you.

Stay safe, lots of love xo.

Printed in Great Britain
by Amazon

84767708R00116